Chaos in the Countryside
Astoria Wright

Faerie Apothecary Mysteries
A Novella Prequel

Chaos in the Countryside

Copyright © 2018 by Astoria Wright

Published by Novelwright Press, LLC
http://www.novelwright.com

Cover Art by Viyiwi
https://www.fiverr.com/viyiwi

First Round Editing by Tiffany Shand
https://eclipseediting.com

Final Editing by 529 Books
www.529books.com
Editors: Lisa Cerasoli and Adrian Muraro

Table of Contents

To my family and friends:
Your encouragement means the world to me.

Chapter 1

Chaos Comes to Town

Thunder, lightning, and rain clattered down on the town of Moss Hill when a package arrived at the doorstep of the Seelie Tree Apothecary shop in the middle of the night. The special-delivery service truck squeaked its wheels and jolted to a stop. A man in a long overcoat and hat jumped out of the running vehicle. He ran up to the door and haphazardly tossed the brown box marked "Fragile." It spun before landing with a thud in front of a set of ocean-blue doors.

Positioned halfway under the roof and half-exposed to the elements, the parcel took a beating from the fat raindrops. It sat still while the car squealed away. Then, without any noticeable outside force, the unassuming, little box slid. It inched its way toward the building until it was covered by the top of the doorframe and protected from the rain. In the dead of the summer night, the flickering streetlamp was not enough for anyone to see it.

Under cardboard and paper, the contents of the package, a young sprig of a chocolate cosmos plant, wilted. But the flora was not alone. Clinging to the stem, a minuscule, tan-skinned nature faerie in an earth-colored frock stood upright, kicking the soil off her feet. A light flickered from her hands, and she patted the stalk the way one might pat a horse, with a gentle caress.

Soon, the plant strengthened to a vibrant green, beautiful despite the harsh treatment it had received on its voyage. Unfortunately, its guardian could not keep herself as healthy. She snorted a loud *"Achoo!"* that no human ears could perceive as more than the usual, tinkling sound of any trooping faerie's communications. The sneeze knocked her down on her bottom, so she was sitting again in the dirt, now rubbing a bruise and wiping her nose.

The wind whipped right through the brown covering. Chaos hugged her knees and leaned against the chocolate cosmos. The sound of rain settled into the menacing drip of water falling from the rooftop to the pavement, too close to the package for comfort.

Chaos' tears welled to the point of overflowing. All she could see was a dim light overhead to her left, an inconsistent light source. It wasn't the warm, unwavering sun of home. *Ah, home, with its sandy beaches and tall, thin trees stretching toward bright blue skies.* Chaos had never known she could miss it so much. She closed her eyes and cried. *Is this what Ms. Corvus meant by an adventure?* she thought.

Eventually, the downpour dropped off. The pitter-patter of rain became a lullaby, and Chaos fell asleep, dreaming sweet dreams of home and nightmares of what was yet to come to Moss Hill.

It wasn't until hours later that she heard the sound of the street outside coming to life. Cars drove past, passersby said good morning, and shopkeepers opened their doors to invite in the new day. Inside the package, Chaos woke and stood hopefully, clinging to the chocolate cosmos and waiting for one shopkeeper in particular to arrive.

* * *

AROUND HALF PAST EIGHT, Carissa Shae turned the corner of Greenfield and Gorse Streets. The wind flew through Carissa's auburn locks until she slowed her pace and finally stopped at her destination. The thin, brown-eyed woman with almost imperceptibly pointed ears hopped off her bicycle and walked the last few steps to her shop.

The lamppost near the entrance to the Seelie Tree Apothecary, lighting the only natural medicine pharmacy in Moss Hill, was as close to a bicycle stand as the town had near Carissa's store. Although technically she should not be setting her only mode of transportation there, the shoppers and store owners here were friendly enough to know it was hers, and no one made a fuss about it. In this welcoming row of shops, she could probably leave it completely unlocked without it coming to harm. In fact, to the eye of a human, it did appear unprotected, but Carissa used her half-elf nature to her advantage for things like this. She kicked the stand of the bicycle open and summoned her elf-light ability to adhere the wheels and stand to the ground.

She turned to go inside and saw a package sitting on the ground by her door. "What's this?" she murmured.

"Talking to yourself again?" A brown-haired woman in a light blue coat, two coffees in hand, came up the sidewalk from the eatery next door. Now serving breakfast, the shop filled the air around it with the scent of fresh croissants and donuts.

"Copying my style?" Carissa gestured at Maren's clothes and her own quarter-sleeve dress shirt, also blue today. She reached down to pick up the parcel, and Maren handed her the delicious, cocoa-scented liquid. She tucked the package under her arm and accepted the steaming-hot mocha.

"I think this is your coat, now that you mention it. You let me borrow it last time I was over at your house on a rainy day."

Carissa unlocked the door, and the two stepped in. "Do I not pay you enough for a raincoat of your own?" Carissa chided with a smirk and flipped the lights on.

"Oh, Cari," Maren said in a mock-annoyed tone, shaking her head. "Do you know how expensive coffee is getting now?" They laughed. Then, Maren's eye caught sight of the package. "What's that?"

"I don't know." Carissa reached the counter at the back of the store and set the bundle down.

Maren didn't wait as Carissa went to the back storeroom and hung her coat up on the rack. She examined the package carefully. "Mexico? Interesting, who do you know in Mexico?"

"No one." Carissa came around the corner again.

"Well, open it." Maren sipped her coffee and waited.

Chaos in the Countryside

Carissa smiled at her ever-impatient assistant. "Okay, let's see." She took a pair of scissors from a cubby hole on the shelves behind her and cut the package.

Maren peered over the top as she pried the box open. "A plant?"

"Looks like it." As Carissa pulled it all the way out of the box, a note fell to the counter.

Maren grabbed the now-empty box, turning it in her hands. "But there are no holes. How can a plant survive a trip from Mexico to here with no holes?" It was a good question, considering their tiny island west of the United Kingdom could not have been a short journey.

Carissa heard her but didn't take in the words. She was focused on the note. She read it silently:

> *Carissa Shae,*
> *Moss Hill is in danger. I have chosen you for the task of its protection. There are fae there to help you and fae coming whom you would rather not meet. Chaos knows them all. Keep her safe and let her guide you.*

Maren glanced over her shoulder. "Raven Corvus? Who's that?"

"I have no idea." Carissa folded the note too quickly, racing both her rising heart rate and her assistant's prodding eyes.

There was no need to scare Maren the way the note was frightening her. She had no idea who this Raven was, but she knew there were such things as fae no one would like to meet: the unseelie. Evil faeries, the unseelie were those who had chosen a dark path of hate, those who found amusement in using their powers to torment others. Cari had never met one before, but the older fae folk in their village in Mount Vale remembered a time long before Moss Hill had been created, when the seelie and unseelie courts had decided to split. The good-natured fae, the seelie, had banished the last of the unseelie from the town more than two hundred years ago. Could one have somehow returned?

Carissa felt her elf-light coursing through her veins and closed her eyes, breathing to relax. Out through her nose went her fear, in through her mouth the stress-reducing mocha to soothe her nerves. There was no sense worrying about a piece of paper. Besides, the note might only have been a prank. The mocha's calming effect didn't last long. A feeling churning in the pit of her stomach strongly suggested it wasn't a joke. She bit her lip, staring at the folded paper in her fingers.

"What did the note say?" Maren called out.

Carissa looked up and glanced around for her assistant. Where was she? The backroom, probably, to put down her purse. When Maren came back out, her placid, unexpressive face and nonchalant tone were likely meant to show she hadn't noticed Carissa hiding the contents of the note from her. But Cari wasn't fooled.

She knew how it bothered Maren when Carissa, or anyone, kept things private from her. But just because Maren poured her heart out the way a barista poured coffee, steaming with details and covered in emotional froth, that didn't mean Carissa had to serve up her secrets on Maren's order. Some things were personal. This particular thing was just plain weird.

Even if she wanted to share it, what would Maren do with the information? Tell everyone she knew, that's what—even if she promised not to say a word. So, Carissa said the first thing that came to mind.

"The plant's supposed to help me with something, I guess." Carissa turned to the plant. It wasn't a lie. Her fae nature made it hard for her to tell lies. The best she could ever manage was a half-truth.

"Help how? Does it have healing properties?" Maren asked, walking over and putting her elbows on the counter to get a better look at the plant. The flower was just a bud. The sepals protruded around a ball of folded, dark red petals. "I don't recognize it."

"I do." Carissa slid the plant closer to her assistant. "You can tell by the scent."

Maren leaned in, closing her eyes and taking in the aroma. "Mmm." Her eyes popped open and she grinned. "It smells like chocolate."

Carissa smiled. "A chocolate cosmos, to be exact. They're native to Central America." Her eyes lingered on the plant. When she finally did look up, Maren gave her that tilted head, sideways-slanted-lip stare that Cari hated.

"You're looking at it like you're expecting it to speak, which I'm fairly certain isn't one of your elvish superpowers."

Carissa rolled her eyes. "Of course not."

Maren, apparently deciding that was enough talk about the eccentric but not overly exciting package, went to the backroom, which also served as an office. As she grabbed some items for restocking, Carissa leaned closer to the plant. Maren was right. A plant couldn't survive a trip overseas without air or sunlight.

"Alright," Cari whispered. She touched the stem gently, coaxing, "Come on out. It's Okay."

A little person, no bigger than her index finger, emerged from the ground near the stem. Her small stature and clothing, which blended with the soil, had allowed her to go unnoticed. The outline of her transparent wings could barely be seen. They had a tinge of red in them, like the flower. Even her eyes were the same green as the plant. They were two shining, round orbs looking up at the giant above her.

"So, you're Chaos, I'm guessing?" Carissa asked. Hesitantly, the little sprite nodded.

"Amazing!" Maren had snuck up behind Cari. In one hand, the assistant had her coffee, and in the other, a carton of vitamins. She stood with her mouth hanging open. Maren splashed the coffee down, which startled Chaos into flight. "Oh, sorry!"

Carissa thought it was time to reel in Maren's wide-eyed befuddlement. She explained in a soft voice, so as not to scare Chaos, "She's a nature faerie, also called a sprite. They stay with plants and other elements of nature to help them thrive and grow. They're thought to change the colors of the leaves in fall and to nurture gardens and tend to flowers."

"Carissa." Maren's eyes expanded to stress her point. "I'm a Mossie, remember? It's not like I've never heard of a sprite. I've just never seen one before."

Maren put a finger out to the plant, and her expression softened to one more serene and inviting. Carissa didn't know what Maren expected from doing that. Chaos only hugged the chocolate cosmos again. Maren dropped it, eventually. "So, she's what kept the plant alive?"

"I'd say so, yes."

"What, sprites can produce air from nothing?"

Hadn't Maren just reprimanded her with an argument about being a Mossie and knowing all about sprites? Carissa didn't point out the contradiction.

"She can control the elements, to some degree. At least enough for a plant of this size," Cari said.

"Hi, Chaos, I'm Maren. Oh, you're so cute!" Maren stuck her face up close to Chaos. She kept staring at the sprite in wonder, which was probably what was turning the nature faerie's cheeks red.

Carissa laughed. Most outsiders would probably say "unbelievable," but in Moss Hill, such things were known to be true. Even if not directly witnessed by all residents, the existence of the faeries was taken as a fact of everyday life.

Maren turned to Carissa. "So, what are you going to do with her?"

The sprite turned her head back and forth between them, breathing heavily.

"She's not a pet. I'm going to talk to her and find out why she's here." Carissa held out a hand, but Chaos did not come to her. "It's okay. You're safe."

The little faerie still didn't move closer to Carissa, though she did drift down to the plant again.

"You said the note mentioned she was supposed to help you. What do you think she's supposed to help you with?" Maren was good at stating the obvious. Carissa looked down at the note. She had no clue what the mysterious sender meant by 'Fae coming whom you would rather not meet,' but it sounded ominous.

Now that Maren knew a new nature faerie had come to town, she was sure to spread that gossip all over.

That gut feeling came back to Carissa, making it clear to her she couldn't tell Maren about the note.

"I have no idea," she admitted. "But this nature faerie knows, and when she's ready, I'm sure she'll find a way to show us."

The three looked at each other. Nature faeries couldn't speak but could communicate through gestures, so when talking to a sprite, one always felt like they were playing charades. It was evident on all their faces that none of them knew what to do. Lacking experience with such circumstances, Carissa decided the best course of action would be to let Chaos settle into a snug corner of the back storeroom.

Chaos made her feelings known by stomping her tiny feet when Cari tried to move her.

"Okay, okay, I'll let you stay out here. But no wandering through the store—stick to the counter." Carissa realized Chaos hadn't left her chocolate cosmos since she'd arrived. The poor faerie must have been tired and hungry. She didn't need a reprimand right now, despite her apparent fiery nature.

Cari leaned down. "How about a tasty treat and some music to pass the time?"

Chaos just looked at her, as if she were unsure whether she should say yes, though the smallest hint of a smile indicated she wanted to. Cari turned on the local radio station, and a light melody played in the background of the store. She sifted through the herbs on the wall of shelves behind her. She watched as Chaos picked which herbs she liked and kicked away the ones she didn't. This new addition to Moss Hill was sure to make Cari's life more interesting, to say the least.

Chapter 2

Customers and Curiosity

Chaos ate eagerly from the delectable flora near the backroom counter, but it wasn't the herbs she liked most. Her curiosity toward the treats in the window freezer at the front of the store piqued when a little boy and his mother came into the shop. The boy opened the freezer and lunged down into it. His dark-haired, cute-as-a-button face disappeared into the cold container so that only blue jeans and two tiptoed, red shoes were visible from the outside. He came back up, holding his prize like a trophy.

"No popsicles," came his mother's sharp reply. "What're you thinking? It's barely nine in the morning."

"Aww, Ma, please. I'm hungry." The boy's brown eyes welled. His face sagged in the biggest pout a child could perform.

"You've just had breakfast."

"But—"

"Timothy Harbridge Jr., you put that popsicle down now." She meant business.

Carissa glanced at Maren, whose face bent into a pout of her own. This was an apothecary shop; she'd told her assistant that a freezer for treats didn't fit with the theme of the store. But Maren insisted a few treats would liven up the shopping experience. Carissa didn't blame her. As the owner, she could've vetoed the idea from the start.

Not only would parents have to steer their children away from that part of the store, now Chaos took to the air, looking at the tasty treat. Carissa put a hand out in front of the faerie. Chaos twisted around, hands on hips, as if demanding why Cari was stopping her.

"I'll get you one later," Carissa whispered. The boy and his mother came up to the counter.

"Good morning, Cari."

"Good morning, Mrs. Harbridge. How are you today?"

Mrs. Harbridge patted her 1960s updo, pressing the brunette strands tightly in place. "Tired. Thank goodness tomorrow is Friday."

"Ma, look." Timmy had his hands up on the counter, with his eyes peering just over the top. He looked at the chocolate cosmos. "It's a nature faerie!"

His mother's lips curled up. The redder-than-red lipstick amplified the apologetic expression. Cari interpreted it as being more annoyance at the interruption than an acknowledgment of her son's observation. "Not every plant has a nature faerie in it," she said to Timothy while keeping her eyes on Cari.

When her son failed to come away from the flower bud, she glanced in its direction. She did a double take, and her attention lingered on the plant. Carissa doubted it was Chaos she was looking at. The nature faerie had sat back down in the soil, blending in well enough with her surroundings that only a child or someone very in tune with the fae world would have seen her. No, Mrs. Harbridge made no mention of a faerie.

Instead, she proclaimed, "Delightful! I thought I smelled chocolate, but it's coming from this plant." Wonder lightened her tone and lit her eyes.

Carissa smiled. "It's called a chocolate cosmos. They're very rare and sensitive. They rarely survive without the help of nature faeries." She winked at Tim, who smiled.

His mother still ignored her son's insight. "I'll take it."

"Oh, no, it's not for sale. Sorry."

"Shame," Mrs. Harbridge said. "It would have gone lovely in the community garden. Though, I understand if you can't contribute this month."

Carissa restrained herself out of courtesy. Mr. Harbridge owned the shop across the street. She and her family were neighbors, which, Cari supposed, by Moss Hill standards, made them friends. But Mrs. Harbridge knew her jibes and used them with less tact than she thought when trying to get what she wanted.

Tim, much like his father, explained patiently to his mother, "She can't sell it with a nature faerie, Ma."

"Oh, alright, fine." Mrs. Harbridge put some money on the counter. "Just the salve and the fenugreek please."

Carissa nodded at Maren to collect the items for their regular customer. She tried not to show her disappointment. If only Mr. Harbridge took better care of his diabetes, the salve would not be necessary. There were several herb-heavy recipes Cari would have been happy to show to Mrs. Harbridge that might help, but she had learned over the years not to give advice to those who didn't want it. No good could come of it.

Tim, meanwhile, continued his fascination with the chocolate cosmos. "I have an anthill like that. I mean, there's an anthill on the beach that has nature faeries in it. I watch them sometimes."

"In the anthill?" Carissa asked. She'd never heard of nature faeries living near anthills. She tried to imagine the ones in her garden hanging out near a group of ants, but she couldn't believe they would ever get that close.

"Uh-huh. They're smaller than the ants. They march like them, too, like they're looking for something. They've been acting a little strange lately, though. It's like they're planning a battle or something."

"Really?" Cari hated that she, too, was now smiling like Tim's mother, discounting the idea. She tried to quickly change her disbelieving expression to one more genuine. This was Moss Hill, after all, and anything was possible.

Cari's senses picked up the bell announcing the arrival of a customer in the Otherworld. The boy, his mother, and even Maren couldn't hear the sound. When Cari's elven senses were primed, she could hear and see both worlds at once. It was a skill Maren hadn't mastered and, as a full human, maybe never would.

But Maren did see the expression on Carissa's face and understood it.

"Tim's taking a three-day weekend away from the haberdashery. The three of us are off to the beach tomorrow." Mrs. Harbridge went on about her weekend plans as Maren came over to them.

She looked at Cari with an expression that said, *Go ahead, I've got this.*

Carissa flashed a grateful half-smile as Maren took over Mrs. Harbridge's purchase. Around the side of the counter, Cari took out a locket from the chain around her neck. The two circles on her necklace, a faerie charm given to her by her father, were set into each other so that the inner one bore a mix of dried herbs infused with faerie magic. Turning the inner circle three times, she stepped into the faerie realm and disappeared from human perception.

Timothy smiled at this, but once again, Mrs. Harbridge didn't register the feat. It wasn't that she didn't see it. Her husband's haberdashery in the human world also housed a fae clothing shop run by a leprechaun in the Otherworld. If ever there were people who believed in magic, it would be the Harbridges. No, it wasn't they didn't believe it; it was they were Mossies, as the people of Moss Hill called themselves. Mossies were used to the fae. To them, this display of magic was mundane.

So, as an everyday occurrence, Cari magicked herself into the faerie realm and looked to the door to greet her otherworldly customer. In walked Miss Morgan. At about three feet in height and slow-paced, with a face that could not cause envy in a woman of any age nor enchant a man, Miss Morgan took her time coming up to the back counter. She was the one brownie who always managed to keep a sour, disapproving disposition, regardless of the fact that most house faeries were known for their helpfulness.

"Miss Morgan, how're you today?"

The brownie only grunted.

Cari, even after three years of running this shop, was still trying to find a reason to like Miss Morgan. She turned around, searching through the pre-filled orders to find the tonic she provided to her regularly. There it was—the yellowish-green mixture of turmeric, ginseng, and a host of other herbs and extracts made to the brownie's specifications. Miss Morgan was the only customer who dictated her order to the last herb. The mix she required wasn't one Cari was familiar with from any of her training in herbal medicine. But, since none of the herbs had a negative interaction with one another, she had no objection to mixing it the way Miss Morgan instructed.

"There you go, that'll be—" Carissa drifted off, noticing Miss Morgan wasn't listening. She set down vial and looked in the same direction as the brownie. Her eyes were fixed on Chaos. The sprite was in the human realm and unaware of their eyes on her. The curious thing was that Miss Morgan could see her at all. While Carissa had full sight of both worlds, she hadn't expected it of Miss Morgan.

"Is everything alright?" Cari asked.

"The note," Miss Morgan replied.

Carissa gripped the counter and peered down at Miss Morgan, uncertain she'd heard correctly. "What?"

"She came with a note, let me see it."

Cari's mouth parted, but she couldn't find the right response. How was Miss Morgan looking into both worlds, anyway? Even if she was referring to the sprite, how would she have known about the note? Dismissing the myriad questions this prompted, she reached under the counter and retrieved the letter from Raven Corvus.

Miss Morgan didn't reach for it, as if she knew Carissa would hesitate before holding it out. It wasn't that Cari didn't trust Miss Morgan—she just wasn't sure what exactly it was she was trusting her to do, or not to do, with the information. What use would a brownie have for seeing such a note, aside from gossip? Although, Carissa had never heard of Miss Morgan blathering, or even caring about other people's business.

She placed the note on the counter, unfolded. Without touching it, Miss Morgan peered down, getting close enough for her old eyes to read. When she lifted herself up again, she scrunched her fingers together. Then, she put her money down, swiped her vial off the counter, and promptly made her way back to the door.

It was the one and only time Carissa had not had to argue with Miss Morgan about paying with money instead of bartering. Her hobbling frame receded slowly enough for Carissa to debate whether to ask her what she knew about the sender of the note. All that business about Moss Hill being in danger.... Why would anyone send a note like that to *her?* She lifted the crinkled paper and scanned it over.

"There are fae there to help you and fae coming whom you would rather not meet."

A chill caused Carissa to shudder. Chaos curled up beside her flower. Her closed eyes and slight smile made her look peaceful as she drifted off to sleep. Carissa didn't mind taking care of a new nature faerie.

But Chaos was here to help someone protect Moss Hill, and Carissa really didn't want a part in all of that.

The bells chimed. Miss Morgan was at the door.

"Wait," Carissa called.

It bordered on rude to call a faerie back from leaving but Carissa couldn't let her go without an inquiry. She freed herself from the counter and persisted to the door. Resolved to pass the note, and the danger, to a better suited candidate, she offered it to the brownie.

"You seem to know more about this than I do."

Miss Morgan's hand did not leave the doorknob. Her eyes left the exit and her nose turned upward.

"It is a note and *there* is a nature faerie." Her nose pointed to the Chocolate Cosmos.

"I know that," Carissa said, "but you seemed to recognize the sender. Do you know Raven Corvus?"

The brownie squinted. "I know the Raven. I know the Crow." It was as close to song as Carissa had ever heard from Miss Morgan and it was as obscure as a nursery rhyme.

Cari shook her head. "I don't follow. The Crow?"

"She had many names."

Alright, that cleared it up—a little.

"Raven Corvus has many names, but who is she?"

"She is a harbinger."

"So, it's her job to warn people?"

Miss Morgan was unreadable.

Carissa scratched her temple. She tried again. "What is she warning about?"

The brownie's eyebrows lifted as if the answer was self-explanatory.

"Danger," she said.

"What kind of danger?" Cari wouldn't give up no matter how much Miss Morgan's eyebrow raised.

"There is only one kind of danger when it comes to fae folk."

Carissa didn't need long to guess. "The unseelie?" her voice shrank. *Evil faeries.* She shuddered at the thought.

Miss Morgan turned the door knob.

"Wait," the word flung itself out of Carissa's mouth before she could stop herself. She pointed at the note.

"What do I do with this? I don't know anything about the unseelie. Why did she send this to me?"

Miss Morgan's eyes looked past her. Carissa followed the stare to the Chocolate Cosmos on the table.

"Because of Chaos?" Carissa asked. "She wants me to take care of the nature faerie?"

It did make sense—sort of. She was an apothecary and she did have the knowledge of herbs and gardening to keep a sprite in good health. She had a whole group of nature faeries in her home garden under her care.

"Raven's note cannot be ignored," Miss Morgan said.

Carissa nodded, "I can take care of Chaos. But what about the unseelie? Are you going to warn the sidhe?"

The hand came off the door knob. Cari had done it now. Well, *she* wasn't going to warn the authorities. What could the human police do against magical creatures? The sidhe, who were the guardians of the faeries, might protect the island's fae residents, but they could throw you in a stockade just for annoying them. And they turned up their nose at humans. Half-elves weren't far behind. Miss Morgan stood a better chance with them than Carissa did.

Behind gritted teeth, Miss Morgan said, "The note was sent to you. She obviously thinks you'll figure out what to do with it. She never bothers to ask me…" her rambling turned into angry muttering.

How was Carissa supposed to interpret any of that? Before she even opened her mouth to ask, Miss Morgan put a hand up.

"Don't ask me again who she is: *You don't want to know*. She may not always send a nature faerie, but one thing she always manages: wherever she sticks her nose or turns her eye, chaos is sure to be found."

Chapter 3

Neighbors and Nature Faeries

The rest of the day went normally. By the time it was done, Carissa had learned three very important things. First, Chaos had been sent by someone named Raven Corvus to help Moss Hill with something that involved a danger of some kind. The second was that Miss Morgan had been interested in Chaos's arrival and knew about the danger mentioned in the note. Third, she would have to watch Chaos's consumption of popsicles.

After a long nap, Chaos had woken around three o'clock to demand her promised dessert and had gone about slurping it up until she'd eaten nearly her mass in lemon sherbet. The result was a stomachache lasting right up to this very minute. Carissa and Maren walked out the door of the shop at four p.m., as usual. This time, however, Cari held a sick faerie in the chocolate cosmos plant in her right arm. She locked the door of the Seelie Tree, jolting the plant. Chaos shook a tiny fist. She then turned and clung to the edge of the flowerpot, her face turning red.

"I've never seen a nature faerie barf before." Maren's neck stuck out like she was more fascinated than concerned.

"Hopefully she won't. It's a long ride back, and all I have is my bicycle." Carissa frowned. She'd never thought about how bumpy it was traveling on the cobblestone streets or the dirt road that stretched a half-mile before she made it to the smooth, paved roads of her neighborhood.

"I'd take you, but I'm still a few hundred away from my future car. Hattie dropped me off this morning, and it looks like I'm taking the bus back home today." Maren's sister was in Nan's poetry group, which had met that very afternoon at Cari and her Nan's house. The meeting would be ending in another twenty minutes, and she'd have to travel this way if she'd attended. Nan hadn't mentioned any cancellations.

Carissa would have pointed this out, but Maren had that look on her face. The shifty eyes gave it away. She had a date. Refusing to look her in the eyes, pulling her lips back so that it was clear she was biting the inside of her cheek, scratching her arm just above the elbow, even though it probably wasn't itching—Maren had the classic unconfident body language she always did when she met a guy for dinner. It may not have been obvious to others, but, having known her since primary school, it was transparent to Cari. She knew enough not to pry. It would only make Maren more nervous.

"Thanks anyway," Carissa said. She tried for her usual smile, but a hint of concern for her friend might have made it through to her face.

Chaos in the Countryside

Maren waved goodbye before taking a step the other way. Abruptly, she lifted her hand to her eyes and looked above the Seelie Tree Apothecary shop. Cari, who hadn't heard the cawing of the birds until that moment, followed her gaze.

There had to be half a dozen midnight black crows staring right back at them. Aside from some shuffling and an occasional flutter of wings, they appeared undisturbed. Cari bit her lip. Birds were just birds, right? So, why did this make her feel nervous?

"Does this seem unusual to you?" Maren asked out of the side of her mouth. Cari snorted at the sight of her friend's barely moving lips. It wasn't like the birds could read them.

"Maybe it's the weather. Looks like a storm. We'd better get going before we get caught up in it." Strange. She meant to say "caught in it," as in the storm, not "caught up," as if there were anything to get caught up in.

Cari undid the fae-spell on her bicycle and placed the chocolate cosmos in the basket. "Sorry, Chaos, you'll have to brave the journey."

Chaos glanced between her and the birds. The sprite let go of her stomach and made sluggish movements between the crows and Cari. She pointed up at them, then swooshed her arm down and out toward the apothecary. She made a menacing face, then a gesture like laughing. Then, her eyes bugged out. She quickly put a hand to her mouth and gagged over the side of the flower pot.

"Oh, I'm sorry, girl. I don't understand you. But that's alright. Let's just get home. You can settle in, and then we'll talk again. Okay?"

Wearily, the sprite looked up again and then nodded. Chaos straddled the side of the flowerpot as if she were a seasick passenger hanging off the side of a boat. Since every bump in the road would seem like a wave, Cari tried to travel slowly on the path back home.

She felt a raindrop on her forearm as she turned from Gorse onto Greenfield. Luckily, that was all. The longer she traveled, the grayer the sky became. But the rain waited until she'd passed the church and the farms and the empty fields. She made it to the base of a small field where the blue and white sign welcomed her to Crescent Circle. She wasn't planning on stopping at the community garden, but a certain strawberry blonde woman in a long, yellow dress waved her down.

"How are you, Cari?" Mrs. Alcott called out.

The sprinkling of rain turned to a drizzle. Cari slowed on her bicycle, wishing she did not have to stop.

"You shouldn't be out here. It's bound to rain at any moment." Cari raised her voice above the din as the weather picked up.

Mrs. Alcott waved a small garden shovel and rake before tossing them into a large bag hanging from her elbow. "I had to get my tools." The middle-aged woman walked to her car on the side of the road and tossed the bag in. "That Miss Carrow borrowed them and just left them out here for anyone to grab. Can you believe it?"

Cari could believe it. She'd probably done it on purpose. Or, if it wasn't her, then it would have been the brownie who lived with her, Gilly.

With the rain now pounding over the field, Cari shielded the chocolate cosmos. Right when she looked into the basket, Chaos fainted. Mrs. Alcott wouldn't have seen it, but Carissa sure did. She'd have asked for a ride if it hadn't been offered first.

Her neighbor popped the trunk. "Better ride with me, dear," she shouted. "Looks like the weather's turning." Her cruiser safely tucked in the trunk, Cari sat in the passenger's seat with the chocolate cosmos on her lap. Mrs. Alcott closed the door on the driver's side with a huff. She looked at Cari sidelong before turning the key to start the engine.

Carissa half-expected a lecture about bringing a plant in to dirty the car's interior. She was too concerned about the sprite to care about Mrs. Alcott's faux leather seats. Cari put a finger to Chaos' forehead. It was warm.

Mrs. Alcott stirred from her silence.

Now Cari was messing with the potted plant. *Here comes the reprimand*, Carissa thought. But no, that wasn't the topic of her neighbor's question at all.

"Are you going to the meeting at city hall tonight?"

Was Cari supposed to know about this? Politics weren't her thing.

"No," she said, but Mrs. Alcott's raised eyebrow judged her into a further explanation. "I wasn't planning on it." The brow went farther. "And with the storm tonight, Nan will probably want me home. She really doesn't like being alone in this kind of weather."

Of course, for Moss Hill, this kind of weather was usually over in an hour and too mild to do any real damage.

"Well, as a shop owner, you might want to be there. Mr. and Mrs. Harbridge, I'm certain, will be to put in their opinion."

Opinion on what? Cari wanted to ask but didn't want to appear completely oblivious. Eventually, Mrs. Alcott got around to clarifying. It was the mayor's new plan to increase tourism on the island. Carissa had heard about that. She wasn't sure exactly what the plan was, but Mayor Belkin had said in his campaign that Moss Hill needed a boost to its economy. Increased tourism would help with that.

"Several of the shop owners are supporting it," Mrs. Alcott continued. "Though I can't see why."

Cari, whose attention had been on Chaos, turned in her seat to look at the driver. "Why do you say that?"

"Well," Mrs. Alcott half-laughed, half-sneered, "I should think it would be obvious."

Carissa could easily have waited for a response, but she had a friend in city hall whom she knew for a fact supported the mayor's plan. True, she didn't yet know what the idea was, because last time he'd tried to explain, she'd only been half-listening. She didn't agree with him half the time, but now she felt like defending him.

"More people visiting means more customers. An increase in tourism would help the town." Cari shrugged.

"If Moss Hill were like any other town, I might agree with you. But with the fae living among us, we're better off as we are now—practically forgotten by the countries around us. Leave our island in peace, is what I say."

In peace and penniless—that's what was likely to happen. Mrs. Alcott had a point, Cari had to admit, but they already had some tourism. As small a crowd as it was, it did help to have the extra money coming in from outside. Up until today, she might not have given any thought to her neighbor's logic, but with that note, she really wasn't sure anymore.

Rather than arguing with Mrs. Alcott, she thanked her for the ride and hopped out. She had to leave Chaos a moment to retrieve her bicycle, but, mercifully, the rain had already stopped. She hurried inside and called out, "Nan, I'm home!"

"Just in time to help me clear the table."

Carissa walked up the steps to the foyer and turned left and down again into the sitting room. The snacks were laid out on the coffee table. Nan handed her a tray of scones. She took it, but not before pointing to the plant.

"Sorry, got a sick faerie here." They rounded the corner up and down the steps into the kitchen. Carissa set the plant down on the modest table. Nan put the trays down and came over to the chocolate cosmos. She spotted the faerie quicker than Cari would have guessed.

"What's wrong with her?" Nan asked.

"Stomach ache and probably exhaustion. She's traveled all the way from Mexico."

"Mexico to Moss Hill?" Nan made a humming sound and pushed her glasses up to examine the patient. "Maybe ginseng?"

"That's what I thought." Carissa nodded in approval. "But I'll have to dilute it, a lot." She opened a cabinet and retrieved the suggested ingredient.

Nan always impressed her with how much she knew. Retired librarians seemed to know a little bit about everything. While Carissa tended the faerie, she recounted the day, right up to the conversation with

Mrs. Alcott in her car. Chaos ate one drop from the little eyedropper Carissa kept sterilized in the drawer by the sink. It was generally used for plant food, but tending a faerie was in many ways similar to treating the most delicate of plants.

When she was done, Chaos fell right back to sleep. Carissa scuttled out to the shed and cleaned out a hanging basket, readying it for Chaos. The night air was a well-balanced temperature, and the sky seemed to be clearing. *It should be a good night, and Chaos might like the outdoors.* She hung the chocolate cosmos on the back wall of the house, near the window by the kitchen sink. Gently, she nudged the little faerie.

"I'm going to leave the kitchen window open. If it rains again, you fly right in, and there will be a warm spot for you on the table. Okay?"

Sleepily, Chaos nodded. Carissa looked up. The clouds were thinning as the sun went down. It wasn't likely to rain again, though even this rain hadn't been in the forecast. Just to be on the safe side, Carissa turned to the rest of the garden faeries for help. She called out, but there was no response. She turned first to the hyacinths. They were still. Next, the roses—no response. It was barely getting dark out. Could the sprites already be asleep? It occurred to her they'd probably relocated to the trees after the rain. She should've thought of that already. She shook her head. Today had really thrown her off.

Stepping back inside, she felt like she'd entered an interrogation room.

"So, what are you going to do about the note?" Nan asked.

That was annoying. It was a good question and an inarguably reasonable one to ask, but still irritating.

"I don't know. I'll talk to Dad, I guess, when he gets back from his trip." The elf historian might have some idea who Raven Corvus was, at any rate.

"Or you could talk to the sidhe," Nan suggested.

The sidhe? Was she joking? Cari had a full list of reasons why that was a bad idea. It started with the opinion she'd formulated over the years that the sidhe had zero respect for humans and ended with the fact the sidhe considered banishment from the Otherworld as a minimum punishment for the mere act of wasting their time.

"I don't think so. If I tell a fae at all, I might tell Rolin, if he'd even grant an audience with me." Cari did a double take at Nan's expression.

The elder Shae woman peered disapprovingly through the bottom of her glasses, resting at the tip of her nose.

"What?" Carissa's defensive squeak was useless if Nan could see right through her thinly veiled excuses. If she was honest with herself, she knew full well she wouldn't tell the head of the elves. She might tell his servant, Sal. He was an elfkin, a distant relation to elves, with pointed ears, a pointed nose, and black eyes. As unattractive as his wiry person was, he was also incredibly kind, and she was comfortable talking to him. Or she might tell his daughter, Hela, whom Cari once tutored on human history and who was always cheerful and looked up to her. But that'd be it.

"Alright," Nan said. "But, since you can't make it to either of them tonight, there's only one course of action you can take. You have to go to that meeting."

"Which meeting?" Cari asked.

"City hall."

"What, why?" Cari hated that her voice reverted from respected shop owner to whiny teenager, but Nan had apparently made up her mind for her. She was already handing her the umbrella in case the rain picked up again.

"Mrs. Corvus gave you a warning. Who's the one person in Moss Hill you have a duty to take that to?"

Ugh. Why did Nan have to be right? Cari bit her lip. "The mayor?" She really hadn't wanted to get involved, but Nan was pushing her out the door.

"Go on," Nan said. "You've not a minute to waste."

Carissa felt her face growing hot as she passed the doorframe. Once the door clicked shut behind her, she was uncertain what bothered her more: the fact Nan had pushed her into action or the fact she hadn't yet had the courage to do this herself.

Chapter 4

Mossies vs. the Mayor

Outside city hall, a flock of birds' eyes glowed as they watched the visitors entering. Carissa felt like she was the only one who could see them until they swooped down from their perch. They were strangely still. Then, something spooked or otherwise set them into action. Cari couldn't tell what had provoked them but was keen enough in her observation to at least issue a warning.

"Look out!" she shouted as the swarm attacked. The crows navigated through running, ducking humans. A few fae were scattered in among them. Some with magic put up barriers around themselves, but those, too, the birds managed not to hit. When all was said and done, the birds had only passed a frightened crowd and hadn't caused any real damage.

Except, Carissa's bicycle skidded on the wet cobblestones, and she was now pinned below her blue beach cruiser. *Ow.* She cradled a bruised shoulder and heard cackling as if laughter were coming from above her. She opened her eyes. Were the birds laughing at them? Or had she hit her head, too?

"Meow."

She lifted her head further to see an upside-down cat. Rather, she was seeing the world upside down, sprawled flat on her back. A beautiful, white cat eyed her with its blazing blue orbs. Its head tilted to one side, as if taking her in. *Scrutinized by a cat. Could this night get any weirder?*

"Need a hand?" a voice said to her left. The accent was strange, American, but it was a human voice, and a soothing one, at that. She turned her head to her left. A handsome man with a tall, fit frame, dark hair, and dark eyes seemed to be the source of the sound. Even better. She pushed the bicycle off her. The man held it upright, then reached for her hand, which she took gratefully.

"Thanks," she said.

"Great eye," he remarked. Either she was still queasy, or he wasn't making sense. He pointed to the building where the birds had been before the flock had gone berserk. "I don't think anyone was hurt, aside from you."

"I'm alright," she said. Hands, fingers, toes—yes, she was alright. Her shoulder corrected her with a sharp twinge. She smiled through the pain. It seemed to work, because the man gave no indication that he'd noticed.

"I'm John." He turned the grip she hadn't realized she still had on his hand into a shake. Now, she was embarrassed.

"Carissa Shae," she said and let go. One deep breath, and she regained her composure. Clearing her throat, she walked with John toward the building. "Are you here for tonight's meeting?"

"I am. Are you?"

"Not exactly." She wasn't sure what to say since she couldn't really explain. In the distance, she could see Cameron coming into view. The mayor's chauffeur wasn't necessarily the right governmental official to contact, but he did see Mayor Belkin every day.

"It's a shame," John remarked, regaining Cari's full attention. "I was hoping I'd have the chance to see your radiant smile again."

His tone oozed charm, a little too much. Plus, she hadn't smiled so much as winced. Carissa couldn't quite stifle a chuckle. It was probably not the reaction John was hoping for, but he laughed, too.

"I'm sorry," Cari said.

"No, I am. I guess I laid it on a little thick."

"You really did."

He looked down, still smiling. The way his eyebrow raised when he looked back up at her, she had to admit, was not so bad.

"You're just so beautiful, I—" he stopped.

Carissa's eyebrow rose higher and higher as he spoke. It didn't seem as contrived, but his tone wasn't entirely genuine.

"This isn't working, is it?"

"No, but I'm flattered that you tried." Because he was staring so intently at her, she added, "Thanks again for the help with the bicycle."

"Well, I know when to bow out gracefully, but it was a pleasure to meet you, Carissa Shae, however briefly."

Her eyes didn't leave him as he strode into city hall, despite her disdain for false flattery.

Her attention diverted when she saw the mayor walk in after him. Holding the door open for Mayor Belkin was Cameron. She hurried to follow, but had to secure her bicycle in the rack first and missed her chance to talk to Cam. She'd have to attend the event now. Maybe she would talk to Mayor Belkin afterward. She'd never been a shy person up to this point. Why was she nervous about talking to the mayor now? Because she was scared Chaos' note wasn't real, and she'd be wasting everyone's time? Or that it was real, and she'd be asked to take on a responsibility she didn't want?

She felt a little lightheaded as she opened the door. She knew which one of those scenarios frightened her. It didn't make things any easier. She gripped the handle, leaning on it and taking a moment to gather her courage. Then, she lifted her shoulders. Standing tall, she entered the gathering.

The mayor was finishing his introductions when Carissa made her way to one of the open seats in the back. No one seemed to notice her late entry.

"And, quite frankly, without an influx of tourism to Moss Hill, our economy will, at best, continue on its downward turn. The Everlys have generously agreed to dedicate a new ship to take the place of the ferries, which we all know should have been retired long ago." The mayor chuckled.

Carissa wasn't impressed. As one of the wealthiest families in town, the Everlys' contribution wasn't a donation as much as a new avenue for profit. But, he wasn't kidding about the ferries. Cari hadn't even been on one, but she knew from looking at them they were old.

Chaos in the Countryside

"I believe with a few more attractions, some restoration, we might draw in more visitors," the mayor said. "We even have some potential investors willing to contribute. This could be the beginning of a much brighter future for Moss Hill. But, I understand your concerns. I will open the floor to hear all of your opinions in a moment. First, I think to truly understand what's possible, we have to hear from someone with experience what can be done in Moss Hill. John? Where's John? Could you come forward, please?"

A man in the third row stood. Cari pushed a strand of her hair back behind her ear and looked away to keep from showing utter surprise. She suspected she hadn't been speaking to a Mossie. Carissa hadn't recognized him anyway, but the first speaker of the night had to be the same John who'd helped her earlier.

The mayor spoke up again. "Who better than a real estate developer to tell us about Moss Hill's potential? Ladies and gentlemen, John Goodfellow, representing MacLir Properties."

The Mossies' greetings ranged from cool to temperate. This would be a tough crowd. John didn't seem put off, though. Instead, he smiled warmly and met the skeptical faces without reservation.

"Moss Hill is beyond charming."

His eyes somehow found Cari. She sank a little into her chair. Was she blushing?

"I wouldn't propose to change it," John continued. "Not in the slightest. Instead, why don't we revitalize the elements of Moss Hill that are most important to the people who live here? Take Fairfield Castle, for instance. You have an actual castle in your town!" His non-Mossieness shone through. Fairfield Castle was nothing but ruins, nothing to get so excited about, "If Fairfield Castle were restored, that would draw in people for sure."

A man in front, Mr. Morely, harrumphed. "It already attracts visitors. It's about the only thing around here that does."

"Ah," John said, "but think how many more that would be if it was a castle they could stay in." His statement sparked some pondering looks. "And the view Moss Hill has at the marina? It's breathtaking. But right by the shore, you've got some old, crumbling houses and a hotel that haven't been renovated, I assume? If those could be redone—"

"Demolished, you mean," interrupted a woman sitting at the table beside the mayor. She said it like she was helping, but the passive aggression in her biting tone and double-edged smile were unmistakable. Carissa didn't see any nameplates on the tables. Had they forgotten them tonight? The whole hall, in fact, was bare. She hadn't been to any city council meetings before. Was it always so informal? It was more crowded, too, than she'd expected.

John nodded. "Alright, yes, some buildings would have to come down. But imagine what would go up instead: modern boathouses, stunning waterfront properties, a luxury hotel overlooking the sea. Every property in the area would increase in value."

Cari bit her tongue. The area was already the location of the wealthiest residents of Moss Hill, and every Mossie in the room knew it. John, apparently, realized it, too.

"And not just the area," he said. "All of Moss Hill would prosper. Homes, shops, you name it. All across the town would be valued property. My investor, Mr. MacLir, is willing to—"

The woman at the front table stood up. She jolted upright, as if struck by lightning. For a moment, she said nothing but looked grave with her pale face and long, slick-straightened black hair. The button-up white shirt and brown plaid pants brought that gravity back down to earth.

Everyone's eyes turned toward her. Cari's brows shot up with her. She didn't know how city hall meetings worked, but she guessed the meeting moderators weren't supposed to make arguments. She looked like she was ready to explode. The woman took a minute to compose herself before making her case.

"You, sir, are not a Mossie, so, with all respect, I doubt you can understand this." She looked around the room. "We aren't alone in this town. The residents of Vale Woods have lived undisturbed for centuries, and we have benefitted much from their friendship. Should we open ourselves to more visitors…." She eyed John with obvious disdain. "We risk disturbing the peace between us."

"Alright, yes, Cleena, good point," the mayor soothed. "The issue right now, though, is the opinion of the people in this room." He held a hand out, palm up and fingers facing her chair. She retook her seat.

John looked to the mayor but attempted to address the crowd. "Well, if there's another group of people we need to be involving in this, I'm sure we could hold another meeting." His words slowed as he said them, eventually sounding more like a question than a statement. Carissa felt a little sorry for him. He was a natural speaker, but the only thing that would have helped him in this room would have been for him to be a natural Mossie.

The room of attendees looked around at each other, unsure how much to say in front of a stranger. John turned to the mayor, but Carissa could hear what he said, given the silence in the room.

"Are they talking about the faerie legends? Do they believe the myths are real?"

The mayor responded by standing and addressing the room as a whole. "You might as well speak freely in front of Mr. Goodfellow. He's going to be with us here for a while, and I'd like to give him our full cooperation, regardless of how things turn out today. Even without the plans for increasing tourism, he'll be investing in Moss Hill either way."

The mayor's admission set off a fair share of whispers around the room. Cari could only make out smatterings of it, mainly a general suspicion of foreign investors.

Finally, a voice piped up, louder than the others. "The people of Vale should have a say in this. It affects them just as much." This was said by a brownie, though from John's perspective it might have looked like a very short woman. She was more amiable than Miss Morgan and more attractive, too, with a tinge of cherry red to her cheeks.

Another human intervened. "The people of Vale sometimes interact with tourists and travel, too. I don't see why this would change that much for them. They'll have more people to trade with when they choose to show themselves, and with more money in Moss Hill, they'll also have access to more resources."

"They can hide or not. They have that choice," another Mossie added.

The woman at the front, Cleena, waited for a hush in the crowd before relaying her strong objections. "I realize I'm city recorder, but I must put that title aside and speak as a citizen. You don't know this MacLir." Cleena's eyes scanned the crowd. "For all you know, he might have plans to destroy the fae's sacred ground with his construction. That would cause repercussions for us all. And if he adds resorts and who knows what else, he'll take away everything that's precious in Moss Hill, and we'll become like the rest of the world. We're a haven for the people of Vale, and we're turning our backs on them because of one greedy buffoon."

Cari didn't know why, but she stood up in response to this almost without thinking. Her face grew hot as eyes turned toward her.

She cleared her throat. Her shoulders squared as her eyes met Cleena's. Carissa realized why she had stood up. What had been said was wholly unfair, and a solution was undoubtedly within reach of reason. She had to speak against it. "I don't think it's right to assume anything about Mr. MacLir or Mr. Goodfellow. We hardly know them. What do we lose by hearing out the proposal, at least? And if we're concerned about the people of Vale, the only fair course of action would be to take the proposal to them. If they vote the same as us, that resolves the matter. If not, the leaders of each people can meet to come to a decision."

"The sidhe do not meet with humans," Mr. Morely said. His arms were crossed, and his tone was flippant.

"But the elder council will meet with Rolin of Vale and other fae. If there's a joint meeting, Mayor Belkin can choose one of the fae who lives in Moss Hill as a representative for us," Carissa proposed.

Mayor Belkin leaned forward in his chair. "Interesting."

Cameron, whom Carissa hadn't noticed was sitting almost directly across from her at the opposite wall in the back, stood up, smiling. "I nominate Carissa to represent us. She's half-fae and perfect. I mean, uh, for this. She's perfect for this task." He cleared his throat and sat again.

"Oh, no." Carissa tried to back down. "It was just a suggestion. I didn't mean me." Was there a deeper shade of red she could be? If there was, she was definitely that hue now.

Several of the crowd chimed in their agreement. Cleena stared long and hard at Carissa, not with malice, but also not at all with appreciation. She leaned into her chair, deflating as the room filled with support for Cari. Several times, Cari heard mention of the Seelie Tree Apothecary around the room, and from a standing position, she saw many of them were her customers.

"It's settled," the mayor said. "We'll hear out Mr. Goodfellow's plans, and Cari will take his proposal to Mount Vale. Moss Hill will decide after we hear theirs." He put a plump finger in the air. "And, if there is a disagreement and a council is needed to come to a resolution, Carissa Shae will represent Moss Hill. All in favor?"

Dread filled her as nearly all the hands went up in the air. There were barely ten for the "All opposed?" She sat, too, as Mr. Goodfellow continued with his plans for Moss Hill. She was supposed to be listening to every detail to recount to Rolin and the others on Sunday, but the thumping of her heart kept getting in the way of the talk.

Finally, when it was done, she walked up to John with a few questions on key details she'd missed. He smiled, genuinely this time, as he watched her approach. Cari's stride halted when Cleena brushed in front of her to exit the room. After she was out the door, Cari exchanged a look with John as both their eyebrows expressed surprise at the woman's open hostility.

"Some people." Cari shook her head.

John's smile widened. "*Some* people are amazing." He bent forward. "I'm talking about you."

Cari laughed. "I could tell."

"Well, I have to thank you for standing up for me."

"Oh, no, no, no, it was nothing." That was too many nos. She had to get ahold of herself. "Um, I just had a few questions since it seems I've been volunteered as a spokesperson."

"Yeah, I'm not sure what all that was about." He crossed his arms and leaned back against the podium. "Why don't I go with you to Vale or wherever it is? Make your job easier, maybe?"

"No." Again with the negatives. "Vale doesn't usually let outsiders in." She wondered how much of their discussion he'd understood. "A lot of Mossies aren't even welcome there. It's just best that I go alone." The truth was only Mossies with either part faerie blood or who were expressly invited by a fae who lived there were ever welcome in the Vale Woods. She doubted any of them would invite a non-Mossie under any circumstances.

"Enough said." He put his hands up. "I can see where I'm not wanted."

Cari smiled. "It's not that. It's just how they are. Plenty of Mossies are happy you're here."

"Would it be too much to hope you're one of them?"

Cari shook her head, looking away. She couldn't shake the smile off, but her expression was disbelieving.

John tried again. "I'll tell you what—I can answer any question you have right now. Or, you could give me a chance and have dinner with me tomorrow? I can answer your questions, and you can answer mine."

Cari's brows knitted upwards. "What questions do you have?"

He held a hand out to pause the conversation. "Sorry, not till dinner."

Cari found he was pushing the charm a bit much, but he was persistent, charismatic, and unlike the Mossies around her. It wouldn't hurt to have one dinner with him, would it?

"Okay," she relented. "One dinner."

John grinned, picked up his briefcase and straightened his tie. "Pick you up at seven?"

Cari wasn't used to being charmed like this. It was a little much. "How about we meet at the restaurant?" she said. "The Second Street pub, do you know it?"

"Sure do," he said. "Can't wait." He winked and sauntered to the door. Part of her couldn't believe she'd just made plans with him, but who knows? Maybe he'd be a breath of fresh air.

"How are you, Cari?" Cameron had walked up the rows to sneak up behind her. She nearly jumped.

"Fine. And yourself, Cam?"

He shrugged. "Can't complain."

"I'm glad to see you," Cari said. Cam grinned. It wasn't in a particularly goofy way; most would say it was cute, but it always reminded her of the Cam from her school days, class clown as he'd been.

Cam put a hand to his neck. "I'm, uh, glad to see you, too. Actually, I—"

Carissa didn't mean to lose patience when he stammered like this, but she noted that the mayor had disappeared somewhere. He'd been talking to some Mossies a moment ago, but as the hall was clearing, he was nowhere in sight. She mustered her courage. If she could talk in front of a whole group, talking to the mayor would be nothing. "Where is Mayor Belkin? If he has a minute, I have something I need to discuss with him."

"He and Mr. Goodfellow are discussing details about the Fairfield Castle renovations." A look passed in his eyes and he changed the tone, sounding more like a chauffeur on duty than the nervous Nellie he'd been a moment ago. "Can I get a message to him for you?"

Carissa led him to the seats and waited for the hall to clear. Once they were alone, she pulled out the note.

"Have you, or the mayor, ever heard of a Raven Corvus?"

"I haven't. I can ask, though. What's this?" He pointed to a little emblem on the letterhead, so small she missed it the first time. Looking at it now, it was a crow, much like the ones that had attacked them earlier today.

"I've seen that symbol before," Cari noted.

"Looks like the statue around the corner on Hillcrest."

Carissa searched her memory but came out blank. She didn't go by Hillcrest every day but had seen it often enough, and she vaguely recalled a statue there. As the mayor's chauffeur, Cam likely drove by it every day.

"What is the statue of?"

Cam titled his head and pulled his lips to one side. "It's a crow, but I can't remember what it's supposed to represent. I can look it up, though. They keep everything in the archives." He took a picture of the letter with his phone. "You don't mind if I show this to the mayor?"

"I'd prefer it." That way she didn't have to do it herself. She stood to leave.

"Hey," Cam said, "I could meet you for lunch tomorrow if you want? You know, to tell you what I find out."

"Sure," she said. She didn't think much of it, and so dismissed the silly grin on Cam's face as they went their separate ways.

Chapter 5

Crows and Ms. Corvus

The cat seemed to be waiting for Carissa right beside her bicycle. Its signature white fur, almost too pristine to believe, glistened in the mist and streetlights.

"You again?" Carissa said. She had meant to chide, but she was a little amused. She unlocked the spell binding her bicycle, expecting it would run away as she moved closer. It didn't budge. The glowing eyes tracked her, though, with intensity.

Now that she paid it more attention, Cari realized there was no owner in sight. "Are you lost?"

She didn't expect an answer. None were provided. But there was a collar. She could see the light shining off it.

Carissa leaned down, now inches away. It puffed out its chest, and she froze. She expected it to hiss, lash out, or even bite, but she could swear there was something of pride in the cat's expression. It seemed to dare her. *"You'll never guess who I am. Go on and take a look."*

Getting over the moment's hesitation, she reached out. The collar itself was strange. It was a golden chain, more like a necklace or a fancy bit of jewelry than an ornament for a cat. The emblem was much like a locket, though if it opened, she wouldn't attempt it with such a peculiar being attached to it. On the front was a fancy script reading, "Aibell."

Cari read it aloud. "That's a pretty name, girl." It was a girl's name, not common to the area in this day and age.

Aibell titled her head. Carissa wasn't well versed in the facial expressions of cats, but she was certain the feline was actually reproaching her for being condescending.

"Sorry," Carissa said. Was she talking to a cat now? She nearly laughed at the absurdity. Moss Hill was a strange place, but in general, crows were still crows, and cats were still cats. Until today.

Carissa attempted to turn the locket over to see the cat's address. She would try to take her to her owners before going home. The cat had other plans.

Aibell pulled away and jumped through the bike rack onto the sidewalk. She turned and faced Carissa again. To be fair, it was possible Carissa had hit her head when she'd fallen earlier, but at that moment, Aibell seemed to make an unmistakable motion with her eyes and head before strutting down the street. It was the universal symbol for "follow me."

It might have been a bad idea—it most definitely was a ridiculous one—but she grabbed her bicycle and followed the feline down the street. Aibell was headed in the opposite direction from her home and showing no sign of slowing down. Carissa kept note of the street signs.

Main, First, Hillcrest? She slowed down as she came upon the last street. Aibell tarried, too. In fact, the cat and Carissa both stopped a short distance away from the very same statue of a crow that Cameron had mentioned. It was a fountain with a large raven, not a crow, sitting in the center. The image portrayed a strutting bird, wings opening, holding mistletoe in its beak, readying itself for flight. Water flowed at its feet, shallow enough to see the coins at the bottom thrown in as if it were a wishing well. The statue wasn't the only thing on the street side.

Cleena, the woman, the one from the meeting, stood by the fountain. Carissa looked down at Aibell, but the cat had disappeared into the shadows. Was she leading her here to the woman or the statue? She watched for a while.

The woman was feeding birds perched along the statue. Three had taken up space on the statue's wing. One was brown, one white, the other a pigeon gray. None of them appeared menacing, but the scene itself was strange. Cleena hummed something, but Cari didn't recognize the tune. Almost as soon as Cari had noticed it, the singing stopped.

"If you're going to spy on me, at least be subtler about it," Cleena.

Cari blushed upon being caught. She dismounted the bicycle and walked with it up to the woman. "I'm sorry," she said, "I wasn't spying. I just hadn't expected to see anyone here." She wasn't sure what she'd been expecting, but this surely wasn't it.

"I wasn't talking to you." The woman turned. "You're Carissa Shae. I recognized you even before the meeting."

"Do I know you?"

"You own the Seelie Tree Apothecary Shop. People are going to know you, even if you don't have a clue who they are."

Cleena barely looked at her. She held some seeds up to one of the birds. It ate straight from her hand. Her dismissal of Carissa changed when Cari spoke up. "You work for the city, Cleena?" She said the name like a question, hoping the woman would volunteer her last name and position.

Cleena only nodded and smiled like this late-night greeting was normal. Carissa wasn't sure what to say. This woman had been downright obstinate in the meeting but seemed content now. Alone with her in the deserted street, Carissa was grateful for the woman's calm temperament. She'd rather not start up another argument about the meeting.

"What are you doing out here?" Carissa inquired instead.

"Just taking care of these beautiful creatures." She waved her hand to indicate the birds. There was smugness in her smile, like she was holding something back.

"Were you outside earlier when the crows attacked?" Cari asked.

Cleena's face fell. She bound up the little sash from which she'd been feeding the birds. "Can't linger around here all night. Things to do."

"Oh, um, okay then," Carissa said. "I guess I should get going, too."

But Cleena had already started walking away. The birds, too, flew off somewhere. Even Aibell had disappeared. Carissa watched the woman until her form faded into the shadows. Strange as the encounter was, what she saw next was downright chilling.

She had mounted her bicycle and had prepared to ride away when it occurred to her that she was already here by the statue. She might as well read the plaque attached to it. Almost the same minute she thought of it, the words on the base of the figure, eerily lit by the lights on either side of the street, became visible.

In a cement rectangle, the etched phrase read, "The Raven Prepares for War."

Carissa gasped, turned her bicycle around, and rode at top speed back home.

* * *

THE REST OF THE NIGHT passed uneventfully. That was good for Carissa, because she'd had about as much excitement as she could handle in a day. She slept later than she'd intended, but at least everything was calm and peaceful when she woke at seven. With little time to spare, she decided to check on Chaos after her first night in the garden.

When Carissa stepped outside, the flowers and herbs were glowing, and the grass was greener than she'd ever seen it. It hadn't rained, but the morning dewdrops added a lustrous sheen over everything.

Stepping to the right, Carissa heard the whispering wind rustling with the movement of nature faeries. They were just waking, and she wouldn't have disturbed them, except she had a certain chocolate cosmos to check on.

Making her way down the path along the side of the house, she stood in front of the flower and squinted. Chaos hugged the stem of the cosmos, crying.

Cari bit her lip. "Come on, Chaos," she urged. "You're perfectly safe here. Why don't you go join the other sprites in the garden? They're very nice once you get to know them, and I just know they'll love you."

Chaos only gripped the plant tighter and turned her head away from Cari.

Carissa sighed. "Alright, stay in your flower pot, in the hanging basket, all the way on the corner of the house, *all by yourself.*" She exaggerated every word, trying her hand at some reverse psychology. Then, she continued, "You're only missing the fun."

One of the chrysanthemums rose into the air, then another and another, with the petals of the flower unfolding to reveal the nature faeries that had blended with the plants in the garden. Their cream-colored skin and tiny, humanlike features distinguished them from the flowers, which their wings resembled.

They swirled around Carissa excitedly. A hyacinth did the same, and one of those sprites flew right to the tip of Carissa's nose, hands out in a question and anticipation waiting all over his peach-tinted face.

"No, I only mean regular everyday summer fun. I don't have anything special planned." The nature faerie laughed and waved his index finger as if to say *you can't fool me.* The other faeries laughed along.

"Really, Hiya." She stressed her point directly to the nature faerie before her eyes. "I mean it. I want Chaos to join the rest of you instead of sitting here alone."

At this, the sprite, Hiya, landed on Carissa's shoulder and faced Chaos, waving his finger at her.

"Stop," Carissa said. "Don't yell at her."

Another faerie, who shared very similar features to Hiya and, in fact, was his sister, landed beside him, wagging her finger at her brother.

"Don't you start, too, Cynth." Carissa put her hands up to take the fighting faeries into each palm. "Make Chaos feel welcome." Hiya looked like he was going to speak. "Uh-uh, no arguments." Carissa put the two on the patio table, under the large, pastel green umbrella. "Be good." She gave one last look to Chaos, who hadn't moved, and headed indoors.

"Those faeries bothering you?" Nan asked. She placed the last of the jam and toast breakfast on the table, along with a freshly brewed pot of English breakfast tea. Nan poured herself a cup and breathed in the aroma, adjusting her glasses on her defiantly young face. She pushed a brilliant silver strand of her short, modern haircut back in place and took a seat.

"Aren't they always?" Carissa said. Grabbing her thermos, she poured the tea in and twisted the lid. A noise at the kitchen window made her look up. Chaos stood in the window frame, eyes shining with tears and a pitiful expression on her face.

"Looks like you'd better take her with you," Nan observed.

"Nan, I can't. I've got a business to run."

Chaos flew over to her, gesturing something. Although Carissa didn't know what it was Chaos was saying, she at least knew that she wouldn't be getting out of this house without the sprite.

"Alright, you can come. But you'll stay in the back room and out of sight."

Chaos stomped, folded her arms, and turned around.

"Fine, back counter then, and no roaming the shop. That's my last offer."

Reluctantly, Chaos faced her again and nodded her acceptance of the deal. She pointed toward the window, and this time, Carissa understood precisely what she meant.

"We'll take the chocolate cosmos. Come on, then."

Carissa retrieved the flower, stuffed down some jam and toast, and headed out to the apothecary. Rather than being sick, this time, the nature faerie seemed to enjoy the long trek down to the shop. When they got there, they were met by an excited leprechaun.

Cari slowed the bicycle to a stop and greeted her neighbor. The leprechaun, named Barnaby, owned the faerie apparel shop across the street. In the human world, it was the haberdashery *Harbridges,* but in the Otherworld, for fae customers only, it was the aptly named *Barnaby's.*

"Morning, Barnaby."

"Carissa, it's just awful news." The leprechaun wrung his hands as he spoke.

"What is?" Cari titled her head as she secured her bicycle to the ground with her elf-magic.

"Timothy was playing by the anthill, despite his father telling him to come away, and I did warn him the abatwas were not always friendly, but he didn't listen. They went down to the beach early this morning at sunset, and the darn things attacked him straight away."

"Abatwas?" Cari hadn't heard the word before, "You mean he was bitten by the ants?"

"Not ants, Cari. Abatwas. That's what they're called where they're from, anyway. Your dad told us all about them from his last trip, don't you remember?" She didn't, but Barnaby didn't wait for her to recall anyway. "They're minuscule, tiny faeries that live among ants. They ride them into war. They're always battling each other."

"Is Tim okay?"

"He's been taken to the hospital. It's not too bad, though. They said he'd be alright in a few days. I was with them up till now, but there was nothing I could do, so I thought I might as well come to the shop."

Cari was relieved to hear it, but given the note and the strange occurrences yesterday, this attack couldn't just be a coincidence. Cari had never known anything like those faeries to exist in this area. Why were they here? Did it have anything to do with Mrs. Corvus' warning?

"What would these abatwas be doing in Moss Hill?" Cari asked.

Barn shrugged. "Came in on one of the ferry boats maybe? Or someone brought over an ant farm and didn't realize there were faeries in it? I've no idea. I put some of my magic around the area to keep others back. But someone will eventually have to tell the sidhe guard. I thought…."

"You thought I would do it?"

"Would you?"

"Oh, Barn, why can't you?"

"They don't like me very much. The sidhe think I'm a public nuisance, or I was in my youth. Lost a bit of my reputation in those days, but I'm very much respectable now. I tell you, the sidhe don't forget anything, they—"

"Alright," Carissa jumped in. She would have done just about anything to make him stop rambling on. "I'll tell the guard on my way to Vale tomorrow."

"Thanks, Cari. I knew I could count on you," he said.

That was just the problem. Everyone seemed to be counting on Carissa these days. But why? What was coming to Moss Hill that was so terrible it would prompt a note like the one from Raven Corvus? And what did she expect Carissa to do about it?

Chapter 6

Dates and Disasters

Nearly the minute her assistant walked through the door, Carissa could tell Maren's date hadn't gone well. She trudged in, shoulders sagging, and said a meek hello without lifting her eyes from the floor. The backroom may as well have been a mile away at the pace she was going.

Carissa pressed her lips into a frown. Her eyes followed her friend across the room until Chaos floated up beside her. Chaos faced her furrowed brow toward Cari and tilted her head just enough that Carissa realized she was about to break her agreement to stay at the back counter. Carissa opened her mouth, without a single word flowing out before the faerie zipped away. A streak of light was all she left behind.

Cari pulled her jaw back into a smile, glad the faerie was getting along with Maren, at least. The hint of a laugh played at her lips as she realized someone had gotten the faerie to visit the backroom. It wasn't long, though, before Maren came out.

"Thanks, Chaos." Maren smiled. Whatever cloud hung over her started to clear. With a cute little nature faerie hugging her neck, how could it not?

"Feeling better?" Cari asked.

A long sigh flowed from her friend. "I had a date last night."

No big revelation there, but Carissa did her best to twitch an eyebrow and tilt her chin toward Maren as if hearing something new. "Did you?" She would have also asked how it went, but she'd hear about it anyway.

"Blind date. Don't you hate those? Mr. Greer's nephew from the Aisling side of town."

If it was the librarian's nephew, Maren's sister, Hattie, would have set that up. Since he lived near Aisling Mountain, he was from the seaside, and therefore a wealthier Mossie. Cari kept listening as Maren narrated his humblebragging, backhanded politeness, and lack of patience with the waiter. She ended on a high note.

"He said I was 'adorable' and would love to go out again."

When Maren jerked her head on 'adorable,' Chaos seemed to lose her balance, but Cari realized she was only rolling forward in a fit of laughter. For some reason, the sprite thought Maren's irritation was hysterical. Or it was a tactic, because seeing the sprite guffawing in the air succeeded in making them all laugh.

"Well, at least you put yourself out there."

"True." Maren walked over to the counter, grabbing the spray to wipe it down while Cari turned on the tablet that worked as their register and record keeping system. "You could do more of that. Work isn't supposed to be your whole life."

Carissa's lips tightened as she suppressed a smile.

Her elfish face didn't escape Maren's notice. "You did go out with someone, didn't you? Tell me!"

Cari cleared her throat. It didn't help that her cheeks blushed redder than her hair as she told Maren about John and the meeting last night.

"Increase tourism? Hmm, sounds good. Maybe it'll bring in more men like John." She flashed her eyes wide, teasing. Then with a laugh, she added, "Who knows? Maybe even one for me."

Carissa only shook her head at Maren and made her way toward the shop door, opening for the day. Business was a little slow, though steady, and Chaos was getting fidgety. Twice, she floated up to the shelves behind the counter, messing with the herbs and tonics there. Carissa called her down both times, but as long as Chaos followed the rule of staying near the counter, Cari didn't mind too much. This changed when she heard a crash and turned to see broken glass and liquid all over the floor.

"Chaos!" she admonished in a harsher tone than she intended. She picked up the shard of glass with the label attached. Her hair fell into her face, but she was able to make out the handwritten tag. Just what she needed— a difficult-to-reproduce order for a patient coming in tomorrow. The faerie zoomed back to the chocolate cosmos and attempted to hide on the other side of the stem.

"I'll clean it up," Maren offered.

"Thanks," Carissa muttered. Then, she released a breath and let go of her irritation. "I'm sorry, Chaos. I didn't mean to yell." She walked around the corner and crouched over the chocolate cosmos. Chaos spun around the plant, refusing to face her again. Carissa straightened and tapped her fingers on the counter. She'd have continued her apology if not for Cameron walking in.

Carissa turned. She caught his eye.

He smiled and gave a slight nod. "Are you ready?"

She blew her hair out of her way and looked up at the clock hanging on the side wall. Lunchtime had snuck up on her. "In a minute." She gave one last frown to Chaos, who was still ignoring her, and made her way to the little hall in the back of the shop.

Maren's head popped over the counter from where she had knelt to pick up the glass. She hopped over the shards in the dustpan and followed Cari into the backroom. "You didn't say anything about a date with Cam."

Carissa took her purse off the rack by the backroom door. She turned around and looked at Maren with raised eyebrows.

"I don't have a *date* with Cam." She pushed her hair behind her ear. "I'm meeting with him about the note from Raven Corvus. I told you, I went to city hall to talk to the mayor and ended up asking Cam to look into it."

Maren held her face in that look that Cari hated. Her tight-lipped skepticism and insistent eyes called foul on Carissa's words.

Cari whispered, "It's not a date." She brushed past Maren out to the counter. Cameron, who'd been leaning forward and inspecting the chocolate cosmos, perked up when he saw her turn the corner. He smiled warmly as she approached.

"Tell him that," Maren said behind her, not in a whisper at all.

Confusion briefly touched Cam's cognac-brown eyes, and he paused. The hint of a smile still graced his lips. "Tell me what?"

"Nothing." Carissa fought the urge to roll her eyes, though she might not have succeeded. She didn't turn around. She wanted to give Maren a sharp look. Cam was just a friend. The goofy kid from school who used to make even the teachers laugh, not someone serious when it came to things like being a boyfriend. "Can you watch Chaos while I'm gone?"

The sprite had nearly blended in with the plant. Chaos wouldn't be hearing any apologies and, though Carissa felt a little sorry for being stern with her earlier, it was the nature faerie's fault in the first place.

With too much enthusiasm, Maren replied, "Absolutely."

As a chauffeur, Cameron seemed to have formed a habit of opening doors for people. Despite it being Saturday and, Carissa assumed, his day off, the mayor's black Mercedes was parallel parked in front of her shop.

"Isn't the mayor missing his car?"

Cam put a hand to the back of his neck. "I'm pretty much always on call, but he lets me use it whenever I'm not needed, within reason." He shrugged, straightening to his full height. "It's one of the bonuses of the job." His smile widened when he saw Cari smiling. It was polite interest on her part, but the awkward pause on his part made her wonder if he hadn't taken it some other way.

He cleared his throat. "So, where would you like to go?"

She pointed with her thumb to her left. The building right next door, on the corner of Gorse and Greenfield, was one of her favorites in town. "I thought we could go to the Gooseberry."

Gooseberry Café was an eclectic mix of red booths, glossy wood tables, and diamond-checkered flooring. Its fresh-baked bread and pastries wafted right through the air such that many entering the Seelie Tree Apothecary ended up lured into the café. This often included Carissa and Maren. Cari's favorite seat was a booth by the window right near the entrance. They settled right into it after ordering.

"So," Cameron said after thanking the waiter for bringing their food so quickly. "I looked through the archives. The symbol is attached to Badb Catha, the Battle Crow. She's sometimes associated with a goddess, sometimes a priestess, and sometimes even a ban sidhe."

Ban sidhe, a.k.a. a banshee. Though, dealing with any kind of sidhe gave Cari reservations.

"What about a raven?" She swallowed a bite of panini and told Cameron about the statue and its inscription: *The Raven Prepares for War.*

Cameron hadn't quite anticipated the length, or rather shortness, of her retelling. He was still chewing and now holding up a finger for her to be patient with his response. Finally, finishing his bite, he said, "That makes sense. In stories, she's sometimes in the form of a crow and sometimes a raven. But, Cari, in all the stories, she's said to be a harbinger of war or death. That note—I'd take it seriously."

Carissa felt almost as sick as Chaos had been yesterday.

Harbinger.

Miss Morgan had used that exact word.

Carissa wiped her mouth with her napkin slowly and folded her arms over her stomach. She leaned into the soft backing of the booth, thinking. *So, a harbinger of death sent a warning note to the owner of an apothecary shop telling her to prepare for danger. Then, she sent a measly faerie, cute but hardly intimidating, as a means of helping defend Moss Hill? Nothing is adding up.*

Cam wiped his hands on his napkin. He stopped eating, and his eyebrows dipped in concern. His voice was soft and reassuring. "The good thing is, no one has seen her in Moss Hill for over two hundred years."

It was an attempt at solace, and she appreciated the effort. She tried a meek half-smile just to show Cam she was alright. He didn't seem to buy it, though. The way he looked at her was strange. There was something to his eyes deeper than she'd expected, and she hadn't come here to fall into any complicated thing with Cam.

She put her hands on the side of the table, ready to get up. "I think I'm done." He nodded and started to stand as well, which caused a wave of guilt in addition to the sick feeling of her manifesting stress. Cameron had almost half a sandwich left to go.

"I didn't mean to rush you. You can stay and finish if you want."

"No, no worries. I'll just…uh…." He stood and twisted over the booth to the stand by the door with the takeout boxes. His long arms reached the distance easily enough. "There, see?" He smiled. "I'll take it with me."

"You really don't have to," Carissa said.

"What kind of a gentleman would I be if I left you to make that long trek back alone?"

She laughed. Cam held the box in one hand and offered her the other. Carissa hesitated.

"Something wrong?" he asked.

She gulped, hopefully not overtly enough for him to catch it. "Cam, you know this wasn't a date, right?"

A subtle cloud passed over his face, beginning at his eyes and ending at his down-turning mouth. Was it Cari's imagination, or were the top of his ears also turning red? His reply and her ongoing rambling were nearly synchronous.

He started with, "A date? No, why would I think that?"

She ended with, "Right. Why would you? I…it's only, Maren, you know. She thought you might think it was, but it wasn't. A date, that is."

That awkward silence returned. Cameron's hand reached the back of his neck again. "We should probably go."

"Mm-hmm." Carissa bit her lip. Turning to grab her purse, something in the opposite window, the one facing Greenfield, snagged her attention.

After an awkward goodbye, Carissa stood out on the street, waiting for the Mercedes to drive away. Then, out of curiosity, she walked to the corner of the street, past Gooseberry to where she could see more clearly who was coming down the road. Since Greenfield eventually turned up the road to a path leading into Mount Vale, Carissa assumed the object of her watchful eye was returning from the Vale Woods.

She waited as Miss Morgan got closer, then, as odd as it might look to anyone who could have seen her, she ducked back around Gooseberry, standing at the very corner where the wall was brick instead of glass. Miss Morgan passed her by, hopefully without noticing. Carissa felt a little ridiculous spying like this, but what had made her pay close attention before was now clearly visible.

Perched on Miss Morgan's shoulder was a crow, very similar to the ones that had attacked the people near city hall. What's more, the brownie appeared to be talking to it.

"Of course, I saw the note."

The bird squawked.

"Hush now. I know just what to do."

Miss Morgan twisted, just enough that Cari was sure she'd turn around and see her. Carissa quickened her step toward the Seelie Tree, but she dared not turn around to see if Miss Morgan was watching. Whatever Cari had just witnessed, she was sure the brownie hadn't wanted her to see it.

Chapter 7

Sprites and Storms

The afternoon was just busy enough to keep Cari sane. Too much thinking about the note, Miss Morgan, and her date with John would have made her a neurotic elf. It was a good thing that when four p.m. rolled around, Maren agreed to get a head start on inventory and let her get home early enough to get ready.

She hoped Chaos would stay home. She couldn't very well take a chocolate cosmos, not to mention the actual nature faerie, on the date with her. Cari placed the chocolate cosmos back in the hanging basket outside the kitchen. Chaos sulked, wrapping her wings around herself and pouting at being left behind. Carissa recruited Hiya and Cynth to help her out.

It was a little strange that the faeries weren't fluttering right to her like they did most afternoons when she visited the garden. She walked to the hyacinth flowers and called out to the sprites at least three times before they lazily rose into the air. Hiya yawned, and

Cynth folded her arms. Both had their eyes half-closed and were leaning in toward each other.

"What's wrong with you guys? It's barely four thirty in the afternoon."

The two little nature faeries rolled their eyes. Cari hadn't seen them like this before and wouldn't have believed it until today. Disinterestedly, the sprites began to drift back down to their perches. Cari leaned over them.

"Hey." She gently rustled the flowers. Startled, the faeries took to the air again. Cynth shook Hiya to try to wake him. "You guys, Chaos is unhappy, and I could use your help. Could you please go join her? Maybe you could ask her more about her home in Mexico?"

Hiya closed his eyes and started floating back down, but Cynth grabbed his shoulders and shook. He wakened, scrunched his nose, and furrowed his brow, looking sharply at Cynthia.

"Please? I really need you guys," Carissa said.

Hiya nodded, and Cynth gave a salute.

Satisfied the two would at least attempt to make Chaos feel at home, Carissa dashed into the house and up the stairs to her room. Rather than fussing for hours about what to wear, Cari changed into a light, floral, red summer dress.

"Don't you look a picture." Nan sat reading on the sofa in the sitting room but peeked through the glasses at the tip of her nose when Carissa stepped into the foyer.

"Thanks. Still alright if I borrow the car?" Cari didn't like driving, but in her dress, and with the distance to Second Street, it was the more practical option.

"It's fine. I'm not going anywhere." Nan flipped the page of her book, but then seemed to decide on inquiring more. She adjusted her glasses and fixed her eyes on Carissa. "I would think Cameron would pick you up. Where are you meeting him, anyway?"

Carissa couldn't keep her eyebrows down. Why would Nan assume it was Cameron she was meeting tonight? Her expression settled back down when she realized she hadn't explained about John, though Nan might have heard through the small-town gossip that Cameron had stopped by the apothecary shop to see her for lunch.

"Oh. No, Nan, it's not Cam. I, um...." Why was she hesitating? "I met someone last night. He spoke at the city hall meeting."

Up went Nan's right eyebrow, which always indicated something was wrong. "The real estate man?"

Moss Hill never failed to spread news faster than wildflowers could grow. Carissa let out a short breath— not quite a sigh, not quite an appreciative gesture. "The real estate man has a name. It's John Goodfellow."

"Goodfellow, you say?" Nan laid the book flat in her lap and looked out the window, as if thinking.

Carissa retrieved the car keys hanging by the door, saying, "He's nice and very charming and successful and just all around...." She searched for the word. "A good catch."

Nan's lips thinned as if she saw right through her. "You must like him very much."

"I—I do." She opened the door, then closed it again, turning back to Nan. "Why do you say that?"

"Because you just rattled off a list of qualities you couldn't have cared less for in all the time I've known you, and yet." Nan picked up her book. "You're quick to defend your choice to go out with him."

"Why shouldn't I?"

"My dear." she stared point blank. "Who in this room is saying you shouldn't?" Once it was apparent Cari had no response to this, her grandmother turned her attention to the book again. Nan pulled her glasses back down to see the writing. Better that than her reading the innermost thoughts written all over Carissa's face.

Passing the doorway and out to the car, Cari debated whether she should go out with John. As she drove, the sky darkened, and the world took on that eerie hue that came before a storm. Thank goodness she'd brought the car tonight. Carissa finally decided it was only one date and far too late to cancel. She brushed aside Nan's words and parked. Going into the restaurant, she took a deep breath and let it go, shaking off any hesitation.

She put a smile on her lips and opened the door, perusing the room until her vision came to rest on John. Like a gentleman, he rose and waved from a table near the front. She was glad to see he was smiling, seemingly sincerely, as she reached the table and sat down.

"You look lovely," John observed. She'd expected him to say that, but he added, "If I'd known Moss Hill had such beauty in it, I'd have visited much sooner."

Carissa looked away and folded her arms on the table edge. She may have blushed despite herself, but she couldn't hold in the slight back and forth of her chin.

"I'm doing it again, aren't I?" John said.

She glanced at him, smiling, and nodded. She tried to keep in a chuckle. "It's not that it's not flattering, but I don't know, maybe you're trying too hard." She shrugged. "Just be yourself."

His eyes shifted down, then back up at her. His expression revealed more earnestness than she'd seen prior. "I'm not sure who that is sometimes." A faint and fleeting smile touched his lips with regret. "I've lived my life for my work up to now. I don't know if it's this place…or seeing you, but for the first time, I'm not so sure of my choices."

Carissa understood a little of his struggle, just from keeping a balance of her shop and friendships in the last few years. It wasn't quite the same, but she could understand how work could consume a person. She felt grateful that she had friends, family, and a caring community to keep her grounded and sorry that he didn't have the same. Cari reached out a hand and set it on top of his. "It's not too late. The future's full of choices. You can always make different ones if you really want to."

John smiled, turning his hand so that he was holding hers now. "Seems like it would be easier with people around who care about you. I've been on my own a long time. I'm sure you have a lot of people in your life who love you."

She blushed. She pulled her hand away slowly and looked down at the menu, not sure exactly what to say. Fortunately, she didn't have to say anything.

John lightened the mood by unfolding his menu and changing his tone to a good-natured observation. "It must be nice living in a community like this."

Carissa nodded and glanced at John. "It's the best place on Earth," she said.

She truly believed that. It was also one of the most hidden and unique communities on earth, which would change with his intervention—but that, she kept to herself. She hadn't felt any disapproval of the mayor's plans before, but now she had a knot in her stomach.

A woman in her twenties with short blonde hair and an order pad walked over to the pair. They made their requests, but Cari didn't feel hungry. She worried instead. Would Moss Hill lose some of its peacefulness once tourism increased? Would the fae decide to separate entirely? She hoped that wouldn't be the case.

They gave the waitress the menus. John thanked her, which reminded Carissa of Maren's complaint from her last date. At least John was polite, unlike Mr. Greer's nephew.

John relaxed into his chair and surveyed the room. "This is the first place where I've seen people genuinely blending in such a tight-knit community. In my experience, that's rare."

Carissa wasn't sure how the place looked to him. From her perspective, she saw a mix of humans, a brownie, two gnomes, and even an elf at the bar. Did he perceive them as human, or could he see what they were in reality? His comment made her wonder.

It was true that even without them looking like fae, the people in the restaurant were all colors, shapes, and sizes. He may have been referring to the diversity in general, without knowing how true his words were.

The aroma of pasta and salad danced in front of Cari's nose as the waiter brought their orders. It was somewhat diminished by the strong scent of John's salmon. Though Moss Hill was an island, she had never cared much for seafood. Still, some of her hunger was returning to her, and the meal and conversation were both enjoyable enough.

John described MacLir Real Estate as an empire. Mr. MacLir specialized in the renovation of older sites, such as castles, and was experienced in the development of commercial sites. He had mediated contracts for a few big-name hotels and successfully increased the attraction of tourists to other small-town areas before. John was the first point of contact for the company, scoping out areas for MacLir to develop. If the leaders of Vale and Moss Hill agreed, he'd set the projects in motion. MacLir himself would only be involved in the signing of contracts and the final stages of the project.

Carissa wasn't sure what it was about this talk that bothered her, but she became less and less certain about the changes as he described them. Moss Hill hadn't exactly been hidden, but most human beings tended to ignore things that were out of place. Moss Hill wasn't near the ranks of mystery of places like Avalon and Tir Na Nog. It was just a quaint little island that, if ever it was noticed, was known only as a boring town with residents who were friendly, if a little strange.

Cari grew tired of John's talk about work after a while. She saw why he said his life was all business. But she listened as politely as possible and only once or twice drifted to look out the window at the rain. The wind whistled loud enough that she could hear it curving around the building. An occasional crack of thunder rumbled in the distance. She bit the inside of her cheek, trying to pay attention to John but also wondering how harsh the drive back would be, up and down the hills in such rain.

About three quarters into the meal, thunder and lightning struck so close to the building it turned several customers' heads toward the window. The rain clattered against the window in streaks of blue. But that wasn't all that caught Carissa's attention. As she peered out as far as she could see, John brushed it off. "Boy, it's really coming down out there. You get storms like this a lot?"

Carissa didn't answer. She swallowed a bite of pasta with little awareness of the flavor. Somewhere in the back of her mind, she knew her jaw hung open afterward. Her ears registered a couple of patrons at the bar mentioning the "soft old day" it was outside, which was a reference to the weather.

Her attention focused on the other side of the window. The streaks of rain were blue flashes of light, and purple, and green, and zips of several different colors. She'd seen those colors every day in the garden. Those were the colors of nature faeries flying at quick speeds. Carissa put down her fork abruptly.

John stopped in the midst of taking a bite, with his fork hovering inches from his mouth. "What's wrong?"

"Do you see that?" Her eyes fixed on the window.

John didn't get the urgency in Cari's voice. He wiped his mouth with his napkin and swallowed. He glanced at the rain and said, "Yeah, that storm's really something."

"No, not the storm," she pressed. How could she explain? John wasn't a Mossie, and even if he were, the nature faeries would never be out in a rainstorm, let alone zooming around like that.

Right after she spoke, there was a thud on the window. A few people looked. Then, another thump. More heads turned. When the third crash reverberated on the window frame, John remarked that it was hailing outside. Carissa knew it was something else.

She tossed her napkin onto her plate and pushed back her chair. Her eyes only broke from the window for a second to speak to John. "I'm sorry, I'll be right back." She got up and strode right out the door, leaving her purse and everything else with John. It wasn't something she'd usually do, but whatever was happening outside had hooked her in. She had to find out.

She opened the door and squinted as a rush of air flew right past her. She could still see the colors, but the nature faeries, if that was what they were, were going too fast for her eyes to see them.

Something in the distance wailed, unlike anything she'd heard before. She almost flinched from the sound of it. Part of her believed it was a person shrieking, and part of her felt it was just the slashing wind. Carissa felt her elf-light coursing through her veins. She held up her fingers. They'd taken on an emerald glow. It was an instinctual reaction. Her body knew before she did that there was danger nearby.

It wasn't just the storm. It was primal, as if an alarm had been triggered in her core. She felt her elf senses kicking in. Her eyes adjusted to a higher rate than a human's.

She turned the locket to the Otherworld. There was the rain, wind, and streaks of light. Though she still couldn't quite see them, she could now distinguish between the little forms and the trails of light they left behind. She lashed out, reaching for a blur that whooshed nearby her. Her hand caught hold of something. It wiggled between her fingers.

The moment she saw it clearly, the shock of it made her let it go. It was a pixie.

She'd never seen one before, but there was no mistaking it. Its eyes were glowing like a possessed nature faerie. Its teeth had sharpened into fangs. Even its fingernails had become talon-like, and Carissa was sure if she'd held on a moment longer, the pixie would have scratched her.

What could have turned these faeries toward their darker nature? The sprites around Moss Hill had always been calm, pleasant, and kind. Pixies were their alter egos, the result of sprites so profoundly lacking hope and so full of pain they chose to destroy what they had previously nurtured. Since they cultivated the earth herself, it was the earth that suffered when they turned.

That didn't explain the weather, but it did go hand in hand. If Cari couldn't find an explanation, she could at least try to do something to help. Some streaks of light fell to the ground. Was this some kind of battle going on?

"Stop!" she shouted. "Stop fighting!"

Her voice was lost to the wind. Was the elf still inside at the bar? Or had he left already? If only she had learned more about her elf side, she might have known how to stop the pixies fighting.

She held her hands out trying to expand the elf-light toward the streaks of light around her. She felt something slashing at her dress in response. The fabric on her upper back had been torn. Almost instinctively, she pushed her elf-light forward. In the immediate area, the lights all seemed to stay still for a moment.

Feeling drained, she turned her locket and returned to normal human perception. A wave of dizziness pulled her clumsily toward the doorway. Her fingers found the edge of the doorframe, and she steadied herself. Once her vision returned to normal, she was glad to see that whatever she had done did seem to be working. The sky was clearing, and the rain slowed to a drizzle.

"Cari? Carissa, are you okay?" John's concerned voice came from the doorway behind her. "You're soaking wet, come back inside."

She might have done so, but she felt a need to do a quick scan of the street with her eyes. Leaves and twigs were scattered everywhere from the storm. But one, in particular, caught her eye. She walked right out into the street.

"Carissa, what are you doing?" John probably thought she was insane. By the sound of his voice she was scaring him, at the very least.

She knelt at the ground and picked up the twig. With care, she placed it in her palm and rose. Anyone, even a Mossie, might think she was strange walking back toward the restaurant, caressing a twisted, gnarled twig in her hands. But Carissa knew enough of the Otherworld to understand what it was she was holding.

This was a dead pixie.

The corpse had turned to wood. As part of the earth itself, any sprite or pixie would become a remnant of nature on their death. It was a rare occurrence, but even rarer as a result of fighting. That was not something she'd heard of happening in her lifetime.

Chaos in the Countryside

A nauseating churning began in her stomach. Finishing dinner was out of the question. She would likely not be able to keep any of it down.

"I'm sorry, John." She didn't try to explain. He was already raising an eyebrow at her, his mouth slightly ajar. "I'm going to have to call it a night."

"Um, yeah, okay. No problem." John held the door wide for her to return inside.

Water dripped from her dress and hair when she crossed the welcome mat on the floor.

"I'll just, uh, get the check," John said.

"Thanks," Carissa replied. She tried to put as much gratitude into the word as possible, considering she was ending the date in the middle for no reason that would be apparent to John. Dripping or not, Cari hurried over to the table. She grabbed her purse and pulled out a napkin. It was a delicate act to respectfully wrap up the twig and place it into her bag without calling too much attention to herself.

John came around the table. "I've asked them to pack up the food. I thought maybe you'd want it later."

"Thanks, but I'm okay." He stared at her with considerable concern, but at least it wasn't crossing into judgment. She really had no way of explaining that he was likely to believe, and she didn't want to cause a panic among any Mossies who might be listening. "I'm just not feeling well. I'd better get going."

She clasped her purse and attempted a smile. "Thanks for dinner." She moved her mouth as if she was going to add something more but couldn't find anything further to say. So, she awkwardly walked around him and made her way to the door.

"No problem." She could hear him say as she left. She closed her eyes, wincing at the bewilderment in his tone.

Of course, she was embarrassed and could have handled things differently, but right now, the most pressing thing on her mind wasn't John. She had to get home. Maybe Nan would have some knowledge as to what could make the nature faeries act this way. Even if she didn't, Carissa at least had to make sure that Hiya, Cynth, Chaos, and the others were alright.

Chapter 8

Fables and Faeries

Back at home, Carissa rushed into the house, calling for Nan. She took out the object of her frenzy from her purse and set it on the kitchen table. Her nan came out of her bedroom in a fluster.

"What is it?" Nan wrapped her robe around her and looked around the kitchen. "What's wrong?"

She showed Nan the twig.

"Pixies, if you can believe it." She explained what had happened at the pub.

Nan went to a drawer in the kitchen for something—a magnifying glass, it turned out, but Carissa didn't wait for her examination. She lunged out the back door and into the humid night air.

"Hiya?" she called out. "Cynth?"

She ran to the chocolate cosmos. The basket hung low and lonely along the wall of the house. The sight of the empty cosmos plant sent a wave of fear through her. It rippled into terror as she rushed down the pathways of the garden. She kept calling out names, looking for any sign of the sprites who should have been there. Seeing nothing, she ran back into the house. The way she flung the back door open, she was lucky it didn't shatter. It did break Nan's concentration.

Her startled grandmother twisted in her chair to see the cause of all the bluster.

"They're gone," Carissa panted. Her eyes had grown to the maximum size her face could accommodate.

Nan's remained the same. "Did you try the old hollow tree?"

She should have thought of that. Right at the very edge of the property stood a large oak the faeries used for shelter in any weather they considered unpleasant. A flood of relief washed over her. Cari's thoughts verged on overflowing into worry again if she didn't confirm the idea. She turned and clutched the door handle.

Nan finished scrutinizing the wooden corpse before she had a foot out the door. "It's a pixie, alright."

Carissa stopped. "In Moss Hill? How?"

"I'd say it was a nature faerie under some type of spell."

Cari came closer, gripping the back of Nan's chair and peering over her shoulder. "What kind of a spell?"

"I don't know." Nan removed her glasses and blinked. Pinching the very top of her nose and sighing, she leaned back into the chair.

Carissa moved around the table. She didn't feel like sitting but lingered around the open seat. A second passed in silent contemplation.

Then, Nan's eyes popped open, and she squinted. Putting her glasses back on, she got up and walked to the sitting room, which housed a small bookcase. Cari followed. Nan's fingers hovered over the spines of the texts.

"What is it?" Carissa felt helpless behind her.

Nan tapped her index finger in the air, still looking but making a point at the same time. "Nature faeries aren't just the sprites. All fae are connected to nature, but some more than others. I read something once about some faeries, a type of sidhe I think, who could control elements."

"It is monsoon season, Nan," she reminded her.

"Have you seen a monsoon create pixies before?" From her tiptoes, reaching over the shelves, Nan turned and met her eyes through the bridge of her glasses.

"I stand corrected." Carissa was in awe of her grandmother. She impressed her often, but she hadn't expected this level of knowledge about the fae.

"You don't spend three decades in a Moss Hill library without learning anything." Nan often reminded her.

Nan's words sunk in and Carissa gasped. "Wait, are you saying a fae is turning the nature faeries into pixies?"

Nan shook her head and tapped the bookcase with her fingertips. "I don't know. It's not here. It must have been something we have in the library." She turned back around and patted her palm on Cari's shoulder. "I'm not saying it's what happened, just considering possibilities. It is a strange coincidence, you have to admit—getting that note, then these odd happenings with sprites and pixies."

"And crows," Cari added. Her excitement and dread compounded at the idea. "Do you know about the fountain on Hawthorne Street—the one with the Raven? Do you think the, uh…?" She struggled. What was the name Cameron had given her? "Badb Catha," she said. "Do you think she could be involved?"

Nan paused. She folded the napkin around the remains of the faerie. "I can't give you all the answers, but I'll tell you what: The library would have more knowledge. " She handed the cloth-wrapped twig to Cari. "Take this with you to Vale. You'll have to show it to the sidhe. They need to know about it. Plus, find out what you can from them. I'm scheduled to work at the library tomorrow. You can come by in the afternoon, and we'll put our minds together to search for some answers."

Carissa hesitated to take it, but she had no choice. She took it and walked over to the front door, laying it on the coffee table in the sitting room. Cari tried to clear the space and make it honorable to the little faerie the twig had once been. In the morning, she could pick it up and take it with her to Vale Woods.

Her next task she almost dreaded to do, though it would be far more comfortable than talking to the sidhe. Still, she had to walk to the hollow tree to make sure the nature faeries were alright. If they were, she could rest calmly for the night. If not, there'd be no sleeping and no ease of mind until she found them.

Instead of racing out the door in a panic, Carissa walked down the path and to the back of the yard. The night was darker than she'd ever seen. Not only were the clouds covering the stars, but the tiny lights of sleeping fairies normally covering the bushes were missing, too. Coming to the end of the lane, Carissa took a deep breath and allowed her elf magic to flow from her heart to her hand. A warm glow resonated at her palm. If the faeries were there, they would feel the magic and not be afraid when she walked up to the tree and peered into the knot at the center.

Closing in, she braced herself for what her elf-light would reveal. She breathed out and nearly cried in joy when she saw a dozen little nature faeries huddled together inside. Right at the edge of the hole sat her two troublemakers. As much as they were rabble-rousers at times, Carissa knew they were also the ones who had led the others into the safety of the tree. They rose lethargically upon seeing Carissa and glided into her open palm.

"You guys, I'm so glad you're alright. You had me worried." She smiled, but no sooner did her lips turn upward than they turned down again. Hiya was nearly crying; his eyes welled like two oversized dewdrops. Cynth looked miserable, too, with both her wings soaked and slumping. All the faeries huddled together with droopy wings and large, frightened eyes.

"What is it?" Carissa asked. She looked around, counting the faeries. Ten, twelve, thirteen, fourteen—that was the right number. At least, it would have been a few days ago. Her eyes scanned the inside of the tree, but she couldn't find the sprite she most wanted to see. She swiveled her neck to face the two faeries in her hands. "Where's Chaos?"

Hiya burst into tears and sat cross-legged on her palm. Cynth's eyes watered, and she leaned forward, hugging Cari's thumb.

"What happened?"

They cried so dramatically that she wouldn't get an answer until they settled.

"Hush, shh. It's okay," she soothed. "Just tell me what happened."

Cynthia pointed, she assumed in the direction of Chaos chocolate cosmos. Then, she took to the air and looked around like she had noticed something or heard a suspicious sound. Hiya flew up higher and waved through the air while making large, crashing gestures with his hands. Cynth put a hand above her eyes and squinted, not at Hiya, but off into the distance. She took off, flying away from Carissa's hand. Hiya flew around her, and she put her hands in front of her like it was hard to move. Then, she and Hiya booth zoomed away. With their show done, they returned to her palm and looked up at her expectantly.

She tried interpreting their charades. "Chaos noticed something strange."

They nodded.

"She flew up a little way." She thought about Hiya's actions. "A pixie came?"

Hiya and Cynth looked at each other sideways and then shook their heads. She'd gotten it wrong. She thought again. Other than the pixies, what else could have happened?

"The wind?" Carissa asked. "The wind carried her away."

Hiya and Cynth faced each other again. Then, Cynth rose into the air and started moving away. Again Hiya came in circles around her, and she lost balance. Cynth started tumbling as she kept flying through the air.

"She tried to fly away and got caught up in the wind?"

The faeries nodded. At least now Cari had it right. But Chaos could be anywhere, and she could be hurt.

That sickening feeling returned. Rather, it had never left, but Carissa had pushed it down enough to ignore it before. Now, she swallowed and held onto the tree bark. It was all she could do to keep from being sick.

Chaos was new to Moss Hill. She didn't know anyone around here, and Ms. Corvus had entrusted her to Carissa's care. The sprite could be a little feisty and demanding, but she'd come on the promise of helping Moss Hill. It was brave for anyone to do, but even more so for such a tiny faerie. If anything happened to her, how could Cari forgive herself?

"We have to find her," Carissa said. "Fan out, all of you." She looked at the faeries huddled in the tree. They heard her. Some of them slowly started standing; others just stared at her, wide-eyed. They wouldn't budge without a pep talk. "I know you're afraid, but the storm is over. If it were any one of you, I'd ask the others to do the same. I know Chaos is new, but she's one of you now. You wouldn't abandon one of your own, would you?"

Hiya and Cynth flew into the hollow and pulled up the other faeries until they had all scrambled out of the tree.

"That's more like it," Cari said. "Now, we've got a faerie to find."

Chapter 9

Lost and Found

They didn't find Chaos. Cari and the sprites searched well into the night. Even Nan came out to help, but to no avail. Carissa would have spent the whole night and into the morning looking, but Nan reminded her that the next day would be a long one. Going to bed didn't help since most of the dreams were about various perils she'd been imagining. Some were wild reaches of logic, others dangerously close to being real possibilities.

With the breaking dawn, the journey to Vale awaited. Carissa rose early, and Nan wished her luck in talking to both the elf master Rolin and the sidhe guard. Despite the former being leader of all elves and the latter being just any uniformed guard, it was the idea of meeting with a sidhe that seemed most intimidating to Cari.

Nonetheless, when breakfast was done, she rose from the table, bid her Nan goodbye, and took her leave. Each time Chaos came to mind, she sped up, and each time she thought of the difficulty of her task, she slowed. It was natural, she supposed, to be hesitant, but Chaos was counting on her. She couldn't let her down.

Just before Gorse Street, Greenfield branched off on a dirt path toward Vale. Carissa leaned her bicycle left toward the trail and skidded to a stop. A small cloud of dirt puffed up from the tire. It cleared to reveal the same white cat that she had seen the other night. It sat staring her down, unperturbed by the fact it had nearly been hit.

Carissa dismounted the bicycle. She kicked open the stand and walked in front of it. "Aibell? What are you doing here?" Cari knelt.

The cat came right to her and purred. Carissa went to pet her, but Aibell stepped away, meowing her disapproval. Aibell stood tall, her regal tail wrapped in front of her like the train of a dress on a person of royalty. This was no ordinary feline.

"Who are you?" Cari whispered. She wasn't sure if she expected a response, but this was Moss Hill, and anything was possible. The cat turned its head and looked down the road to Gorse Street. Carissa followed her gaze. Was she looking toward the shop? Could there be something in that direction that revealed a clue to Aibell's identity? Did it have anything to do with Raven Corvus and Chaos?

In that same soft voice, Carissa asked, "What are you trying to tell me?"

Aibell faced Cari eye to eye, then turned and trotted ahead toward Gorse Street. Carissa sat still, wondering whether she'd be crazy to follow. But just as she thought that, the feline looked behind her and stopped, as if asking, "Well, are you coming?"

Whether she believed it or not, Cari snapped into action. She wasn't about to let this curiosity pass her by. She took up the stand and mounted the bicycle, then followed the cat as it increased its speed down the lane.

As expected, Aibell turned down the corner of Greenfield and Gorse. She settled in front of Gooseberry, leaned against the window, and meowed. Carissa looked, but there wasn't a person in sight. The fresh pastry scent was the only thing filling the street, and as tempting as it was, it hardly merited this diversion from her journey.

"There's nothing here."

Aibell lifted herself up on her hind legs and touched her front paws to the glass. Carissa felt downright silly.

"Is that what you wanted? Breakfast?" She laughed. "Alright, wait here, and I'll get you something. But then it's right back to your owner." She left her bicycle outside the café and entered to the heavenly aroma of Gooseberry. The line was short, with only two people in front of her, since it was so early in the morning. One customer already sat at a booth—one that happened to be right near where Aibell was waiting outside. She glanced over once or twice to make sure the cat was okay. Then, she took out her phone, searching through the contacts to figure out whom to call to pick up Aibell and take her to her owner. She didn't have time today.

But she didn't have to call anyone. Her phone rang. She glanced at the screen: Maren Raines, it read.

"Hello?" she answered.

"Hey, Cari? This is going to sound strange."

Carissa gripped the phone tighter. For a minute, she thought maybe Chaos had found her way to Maren. Or maybe Maren had found her somewhere, injured or worse. She braced herself and told Maren to go ahead and share the news.

"Well, I was just out shopping, and there was a little crowd gushing around that guy you went out with last night, John Goodfellow. He said you were acting pretty strange."

The blood rushed out of her face. Carissa bit her lip before she realized Maren couldn't see her.

"He...." She swallowed. "He said it in front of a whole group?"

"No," Maren gasped. "Sorry, not what I meant. People were crowding around him, and he was answering questions about the mayor's plans for the town. I introduced myself, and after the crowd dispersed, he stopped me to talk privately. He said you cut the date short because you weren't feeling well. Are you okay?"

Carissa resumed breathing. Sure, her behavior had been odd, but at least John was enough of a gentleman not to be spreading the word about it all over town. "I'm fine," she assured Maren.

Maren's voice came in at a barely audible level. "He also said you went outside during the storm, like you saw someone, maybe? Was everything alright?"

Cari's lip twitched to one side. If she told Maren, her friend would think she had the news of the century. No force on earth would stop her from telling everyone in town. No matter how well-meaning her best friend was, she had a lot of friends and little willpower for keeping secrets. She could do fine with the small stuff. But something like pixies on the loose? No way. She'd spill that like a bursting dam.

"Actually," Carissa said. She lowered her voice and backed away from the line. "Chaos is missing." She filled Maren in on the details of the disappearance. Then, she pulled the phone away in anticipation of Maren's overreaction, which she gave. Maren agreed to comb the whole of Moss Hill for the nature faerie.

The first in line finished as Cari thanked her and hung up. A second later, she realized that she'd forgotten to ask about her watching the cat. Moving forward with the line, she glanced again at the window, but this time caught the eye of the woman seated there: Cleena.

It would make anyone suspicious to have someone keep glancing in their direction. It wasn't terribly surprising when the woman rose and walked directly over to Carissa.

Cari felt she should explain that she hadn't meant to be rude. She opened her mouth but was cut off by the woman.

"Carissa, good morning."

Cari gave a kind "Good morning," noting the woman's frown and flared nostrils teetering between fear and anger. Carissa knew they had disagreed at the meeting, but she didn't want an argument here. Carissa turned back to the line and entered her passcode on the phone, so she could call Maren back.

Cleena did not relent. "I heard about the boy, Harbridge's son, and the storm last night. Do you know when he'll be out of the hospital?"

Carissa felt it would be inappropriate not to converse with her when she was asking about a fellow Mossie. When she turned around, it was clear from the creased eyebrows and down-curving lips that the woman was concerned about Timothy.

"The last I heard from Barnaby before we closed yesterday was he would be in a few days more, but he'll be okay."

Cleena's forehead smoothed, as if years were taken off in that second. She nodded. Carissa expected her to leave at that point, but she lingered. The woman's brow jutted down again, and her lips thinned. "I didn't mean to eavesdrop, but did you say something about nature faeries just now?"

Carissa's own eyes widened. She knew she shouldn't be surprised people had heard her phone conversation with Maren. She had tried to be vague, but with Mossies all around, she shouldn't have said anything in public.

"Just...." She raised up her shoulders. "Weird weather." She made as if to shrug it off but ended in something like a shudder as she said, "It's been affecting the nature faeries, I think."

The crinkles by the woman's eyes deepened. She didn't look old by any means, but the worry aged her again.

Carissa hesitated. The woman was a Mossie, so she would understand about the nature faeries. They acted odd sometimes, especially in weird weather. This shouldn't have concerned her so much—unless she'd seen the pixies too?

"Have you—" Carissa started, but Cleena jumped in at the same time.

"Your friend you mentioned, Chaos—is that a nature faerie who's missing?"

Carissa clenched her jaw tight. Say something or not? The woman in line in front of her had finished her order and pushed past them out the door. The woman at the counter, a schoolgirl, named Ivy, called, "Next?"

Carissa glanced between the cashier and the woman. Then, she took a step forward without answering. She turned to the display case and looked over the entrees sitting inside the heated, covered buffet. What did cats eat?

She recalled Hattie's cat loved eggs and pumpernickel. Eyeing them in the silver tray right beside the register, she put in an order for that. While she waited for Ivy to scoop up the eggs and cut a slice of the bread, she was vaguely aware of Cleena still lurking behind her.

"Carissa?" Cleena called for her attention.

Inwardly, Cari begged for her to go away, but she took a breath and steeled her resilience to turn around again. She tightened her jaw behind a close-lipped smile and waited to hear what Cleena might still have to say.

"I know you, and I don't share the same position on the tourism proposal," Cleena said. "But that doesn't mean I don't want to help you."

Carissa didn't think of her opinion as a "position," but being in city hall probably made this woman think in those political terms.

Cleena stepped closer. Her eyes were so dark they appeared black. "I've been city recorder for a long time now, and I've helped a lot of Mossies, both human and fae."

Chaos in the Countryside

It took Cari some time to pinpoint the emotion this woman was portraying. It was a need. Cleena needed Carissa to believe her—no, to justify her.

"If you need help," Cleena continued, "just ask." She waited there, unmoving. Her eyes were fixed on Carissa, whose face was a mask.

She didn't know whether to trust this woman. Ever since getting Raven Corvus' note and all the strange happenings, she didn't know who to trust. Cleena swallowed and frowned, then took a step back to her table.

"Wait." Carissa closed her eyes and broke the tension in her own face. What harm would it do to tell her about Chaos? If the sprite were to stay in Moss Hill for years to come, they might see her around anyway. Plus, she might need all the help she could get in finding her.

Now relaxing, Carissa said, "It's a sprite from my garden who's missing. She has long, black hair, a sandy complexion, a purple dress, and red wings. If you see her, will you please let me know?"

Cleena smiled. It was a kind smile, a sympathetic one. It made Carissa glad she'd chosen to trust her. She'd always been open with her fellow Mossies before. She didn't want Raven's note to change that. So, why did her chest still feel tight? She ignored the feeling and returned Cleena's smile with one of her own.

Cleena, with that same determination Carissa had seen in city hall, said, "I'll gather a few fae and spread the word. We'll find her."

Cari's eyebrows shot up, and she stepped back. She held a hand up. "Oh, no, you don't have to do that."

"Why not?" Her reaction was like adding fuel to fire.

Why not was a good question. The answer was a note—a note Cari couldn't tell Cleena about, that exposed the reason for Chaos being here.

Carissa felt an argument coming on. She did want to find Chaos but was sure Raven Corvus hadn't meant to spread the word about Chaos even being in town. What if a dark fae was in Moss Hill and knew about her? What if they decided to kidnap her? So many questions swished through her mind that she almost missed the flood of fury bursting from Cleena's lips.

"Trust me or not, I'll still help you. We Mossies only have each other, Carissa. We stick together. I hope you'll remember that when you speak with Rolin."

So, she wanted to change Carissa's mind? Or was she genuinely just trying to help? Cleena's motivations aside, Cari still wasn't sure it was a good idea to spread the word about Chaos. Ivy called out to her that her order was ready.

"I do appreciate your help," Carissa said. "But you don't have to make a big deal. Just keep an eye out for her."

Cleena moved between her and the cashier. "Let me be clear—I think you should tell Rolin not to agree to it."

Cari's lips already began to form an argument, but Cleena put a hand up. The gesture worked to quell Cari into hearing her out.

"The mayor's jumping into this without all the facts. He's putting Moss Hill at risk."

Cari looked off to the side, shaking her head. This was the same argument Cleena had made at the meeting.

"It's really not up to me to decide," Carissa said.

Cleena clicked her tongue and scoffed. "Let me be forthright. I don't want MacLir on these shores. You don't know him. I can tolerate the tourism. I've even offered to help the mayor re-envision the project. But, I tell you, Carissa, he's not one to trust."

Carissa bit the inside of her lip. Confusion passed over her squinting eyelids. "Why?"

Cleena met her with a stoic expression. "He's a destructive force. Look what happened in Moss Hill at even the mention of his name." Contempt dripped from a grimace at her lips.

Carissa didn't respond except to swallow, but she didn't look away. The one tiny signal of her fear wasn't lost on Cleena.

"I'm scaring you. I'm sorry." Cleena paled. Something was going on with her countenance Carissa couldn't make out. Was she ill, perhaps?

"Are you alright?" Carissa put a hand out as if to hold on to her, but she didn't touch her.

"I'm fine, really." She apologized again. She grasped Carissa's wrist as Cari had almost done a moment ago. She wasn't sure if it was Cleena's attempt to steady herself or to add to the gravity of her next words. "I only care about Moss Hill, Carissa, and I will do everything in my power to protect it."

A small, reassuring smile on Cleena's part ended the awkward exchange. She let go of Cari's arm and walked to the table to gather her things. One could only wonder what Ivy thought of the conversation or how much she'd heard. Cari paid the cashier for the readymade eggs and exchanged a little eyebrow raise with her before Cleena got her bag and left a tip on the table.

When they both reached the exit at the same time, Cleena held the door open for Carissa. It was a thoughtful, unexpected gesture that only served to make Carissa more suspicious of her true intent. Nonetheless, Cari thanked her and headed outside.

The thought crossed her mind that she might look a little silly feeding a cat on the sidewalk from a takeout container, but she smiled at Aibell and opened the box. To her surprise, Aibell hissed and barred her talons.

"What's wrong?" Cari asked.

She realized she was still standing in the doorway, blocking Cleena's exit, and moved toward the cat, though with caution. Cleena followed behind her. But before the woman passed the door, and well before Cari could reach the cat, Aibell turned. With a flick of her tail, she sprinted down the street.

"Great," Carissa said aloud. She was so dismayed she turned to vent to Cleena. That was twice that cat had evaded rescue—only, this time, she had a meal in hand.

By the time Cari had thrown her hands up, then quickly realized the container was open and swerved to keep the contents in line, Cleena, too, was gone. All Carissa could do was shake her head and place the carton in the basket of her bicycle. Clicking up the stand, she took her place on the seat and began the long trek, now made longer with the interruption.

Chapter 10

Fae and Formalities

With her elf-light, Carissa sped up her journey to the Vale Woods. She raced through the path in the Otherworld, where she could see all the pitfalls and see through all the false images the fae used to mislead normal humans from finding their village. She got all the way to the base of Vale Mountain by the time she had hoped to be at Master Rolin's. The faerie village at Mount Vale's base was situated at an altitude that, in the human world, appeared like a steep incline, too dangerous to climb. From the perspective of the Otherworld, there was a staircase built into the dirt, with only hints of stone and wood as evidence of unnatural construction.

Carissa jogged up the steps but slowed when she reached the top. The pace was easy for a fae to keep; it was the eyes on her when she popped into sight that measured her steps. The fae, out and about, starting their days, didn't keep such a quick step about them.

They all turned their attention to her, startled and wondering what had panicked her into a hurry.

Cari settled her elf-light back down at her core and concentrated on slowing her breath. She smiled at passing elves and brownies, sidhe, and the numerous types of fae on the path. Finally, she came to the near-center of town, the largest home in the village if you discounted the Redwood Hollow that housed all the sidhe. The large, curved, wooden doors of Rolin of Vale's house loomed over her.

She set her back straight, firmly planted her feet on the ground, and knocked. A moment passed before the oversized door creaked open, and she saw a familiar, jovial face.

Before speaking with Rolin, visitors were always greeted by Sal. The elfkin had worked for the head of the elves since Carissa was a child. Happy by nature, Sal had always helped her see the bright side of things. She'd love to just leave the mayor's message with him, but her instructions were to talk to Master Rolin directly.

"Hello, Sal," Carissa said.

"Cari, we were expecting you."

Of course, they were—Moss Hill and Vale were both still small enough for word to pass quickly between them.

"Is Master Rolin home?"

"You couldn't have come at a better time. He's just had breakfast in the garden. I haven't given him today's news yet. Might as well start with you." He reached a hand to Cari's back and moved behind her, gently pushing her through

Chaos in the Countryside

Two steps into the house, Sal sniffed loudly behind her. "Pumpernickel bread?" Was he asking or offering? Then she remembered the container from Gooseberry and Sal's love of pumpernickel anything.

She laughed. Sal removed his hand from her back and breathed in the scent as they continued walking. Without turning around, she said, "It's in my bicycle basket. You're welcome to help yourself."

Carissa's thoughts redirected to the garden as it came into view. The day was beautiful. A mix of butterflies and nature faeries fluttered about the bushes and trees. Whatever "destructive force" had affected Moss Hill didn't seem to have made its way to Vale. The family was seated together on a patio table, made of wood and tree stump to appear like a natural part of the garden. They were finishing their meals with content expressions on their faces. Their daughter, Hela, smiled, as usual.

Cari wasn't sure she wanted to be the first news of Rolin's day, but she supposed he might be in his best mood after breakfast. Not that she'd seen him in foul spirits often. On the contrary, it wasn't that Master Rolin wasn't kind or good-natured. He wasn't one to fear.

But he was the head of the Fae Council, also known as the Elven Council since it consisted entirely of elves. Cari's father was a member, and from what he had told her of Rolin, he was fair but often hasty. He had a low tolerance for wasting time or attention. His mind was sharp enough to know where you were going with a thought. He could pick up on nonverbal cues such as fear or intimidation. If, for a second, he believed your logic was irrelevant or unfounded, the discussion would end.

He might sound intimidating, but unlike the members of the Sidhe Council, Rolin would at least hear a human out. Carissa wasn't sure that the sidhe would even listen to a half-elf if she ever had to speak to one of the elders on their council. In comparison, her task today should be easy.

Sal trotted her out on her heels until she was standing before Rolin, his wife, Mariquet, and the red-haired heiress, Hela. Rolin wiped his mouth with a handkerchief and pushed his plate aside. Sal rushed over and picked it up. Hela, who was inspecting the berries for the ripest one, discarded the whole bunch on noticing Carissa's entrance.

"Cari!" she shouted. At a hundred years old, she looked younger than Carissa's thirty. Human years and fae years didn't exactly correlate, but Carissa pegged her as equivalent to an exuberant nineteen-year-old, if one were attempting to measure such things. She hugged her old student—at one point, Hela had studied human scripts, so she could read and write in English, or "common human," as the elves referred to it.

"Oh, I have so much to tell you. I'm seeing someone, you'll never guess who—"

Rolin stood. "Another time, Hela. I have business to discuss with Carissa Shae."

He tapped Hela's shoulder twice and gave his wife a nod. Rolin's wife lowered her chin to Cari, and she returned the gesture. Hela gave Carissa another hug before gliding away. Rolin opened his palm toward the stepping stone path around the garden.

Chaos in the Countryside

Walking in the fresh air and flowers made it easier for Carissa to say her piece about the mayor's proposal on tourism. Cleena's words echoed in her ears the whole time, but she tried not to let it show. Rolin listened wordlessly, but nodded to show his understanding. It was easier to talk to him than she had expected. He hadn't cut her off and didn't seem to be trying to hasten her through her speech. She was a better speaker than she'd thought she would be, too.

"So, the mayor believes that overall, the increase in tourism will benefit both the human and fae communities," she concluded.

He put a hand to his chin, deliberating. She'd ended thinking she'd done well, but the silence made her doubt her skill in diplomacy.

At long last, Rolin replied, "You've given me much to consider."

She waited. *And? What did that mean? Was it a yes, a no, a maybe?* she wondered.

He stopped, and she followed suit, so they were standing in the garden face to face. He still said nothing, which was beyond frustrating to Carissa. Given his total lack of movement, he might have become a plant growing in the ground.

Another while passed, and he spoke again. "I will take the matter to the Sidhe Council." He turned abruptly and walked back in the direction of the house. Carissa followed. The butterflies might as well have been in her stomach. She was delighted she'd done well enough for him to confer with the sidhe.

A few steps away from the house, though, he added, "You smile too soon. Cleena of Moss Hill also visited yesterday to make the opposite argument. Both sides must be given equal consideration."

Her lips dropped back into solemnity. She tucked her chin into chest, deep in contemplation as they walked back into the house. So, Cleena had already made her plea to Rolin? She'd failed to mention that little fact this morning. What kind of game was she playing?

Back inside, Carissa bowed her head to Rolin and his wife and took her leave. Sal walked her out cheerily. He chatted about something, but she only half-listened.

"And so I said to him, if he's got half a coin, give him half a carton!" Sal grinned at her.

Was that a punchline? His smile was expectant, but she hadn't heard enough to give an appropriate response. If it weren't a joke, laughing would be rude, and fae folks were easily hurt. She settled on a smile to match Sal's exact expression.

"Good one, Sal." That worked. It was an easily interpretable expression and made him jolly as he could be, which, for Sal, was a considerable amount.

Sal said goodbye with the promise to give Carissa's goodbyes to Hela. At the end of it, she was glad he hadn't asked about the meeting. The truth was, after a confusing morning, she wasn't all too sure which decision was right for Moss Hill. She was glad it was in Rolin's hands and not her own.

She nearly traveled right out of the village without another word to anyone, but her eyes caught a glint of bronze shining down the road. She stopped right there, and a fae bumped into her. "Watch where you're going!" she heard, and she heard herself utter, "Sorry" back.

Chaos in the Countryside

Biting her lip, Cari started again, this time right toward the sidhe guard, whose badge had reflected the sun. He was watching passersby, but she couldn't tell if he was on duty; the sidhe guards perpetually wore that disapproving look.

The guard barely acknowledged her until she was standing right in front of him, blocking his path. His slender ears twitched, and his long, blond hair draped to the side as he bent his head in anticipation of her inquiry. "Speak," he ordered.

She squinted, trying to recall enough Elvish to make out the name written on his badge. "Sir, um, Varick?" she began.

His gaze scrutinized her. He inhaled and crossed his arms. "You smell human." His eyes traveled up and down. "Are you the Shae child?"

She took in a breath and reminded herself she was not at all a child and had as much right as any fae to be offended by that statement. She mirrored his gesture, bringing her own arms to her chest. The sidhe, as a people, did not acknowledge or appreciate weakness.

"I am the woman, Carissa Shae, daughter of the Keeper of Records of the Fae Council." *Did she imagine the slight upturn of the right corner of his lip? Was she amusing him?* "And I demand assistance."

It was too far. The upturned lip was gone. Varick uncrossed his arms. Alarm bells rang in Cari's brain. Fae or not, daughter of a councilman or not, it was stupid to "demand" anything of a sidhe.

She dropped her own arms but wasn't foolish enough to look down. She'd lose all respect if she didn't keep her standing after challenging a sidhe like that.

She did, however, need to take it back without losing ground.

Her mind raced for words. She tried as calm and powerful a voice as possible, a difficult combination. "With respect, the speech did not accurately relay the intent. May I request your assistance?"

A little muscle in his cheek flinched. *Anger? Annoyance?* His eyes were still green, so he couldn't be that upset. If the flecks of gold were glistening, she might have been in trouble. But this was a secondary guard and not a leader of a squad. He would have superiors to impress.

While they didn't like humans, the closest thing to respect the sidhe had for any other of the faerie races was given to the Elven Council. As Dorian's daughter, she might be one he would try to appease.

"State your request." He re-crossed his arms and cocked his head again. He listened like a bouncer waiting for management to give the word to get her out of there. At least he was listening as she relayed her concern for the missing nature faerie.

"Her name is Chaos," she finished. By now, he had taken her seriously enough that he was writing into a small notepad. It was a great sign. "She's about three inches tall, tan, and her wings are like a chocolate cosmos."

He raised a brow.

"It's a red flower that smells like chocolate." She was veering. "The smell's not important." She had to stop herself by physically chomping down on her cheek.

"Any suspects?"

"Suspects?"

His eyes moved upward, but the rest of his body stayed poised to write. He explained to Cari like she was two, "A person who might have taken her."

"I don't think...I mean, I don't know if she was taken."

He snorted or grunted or made some kind of disapproving noise in a puff of air from his lips.

Cari realized she'd slid back into her old pattern of discomfort. She was a business owner, for goodness sake. It was this fae world. She never felt like she fit in, and being anywhere near a sidhe didn't help. She expanded her person by filling her lungs with air.

In a steadier voice, she said, "Chaos has only talked to me, my grandmother, and my best friend. No one else even knows she's here." She debated about telling him about the note. Nan had said she should. Miss Morgan had reacted to it. Now that she thought about it, she added to her testimony, "And Miss Morgan. She also saw Chaos."

To this, the sidhe looked up from his writing. The pause was brief. He flipped the pad and tucked it into his shirt pocket. Curtly, he stated her request had been heard and promptly walked away before she had a chance to say anything about the note.

As far as interactions with sidhe went, Carissa thought it had gone well. She exhaled relief and made it out of the village and down the steps in one piece. She chuckled a little on seeing the empty basket of her bicycle. Sal had helped himself to the eggs and pumpernickel while she was occupied. Her stomach rumbled at the thought of food, and she was happy to be getting home.

But the hunger took on a sick feeling as the empty basket recalled memories of the chocolate cosmos and Chaos. She'd just reported Chaos missing, but the sight made it more real. She began the long trek not home, but to the library. Hopefully, Nan had found some answers.

Chapter 11

Books and Banshees

Returning to Moss Hill, Carissa stopped by the library to see Nan. She was eager to find out more about the fae who might be responsible for the odd events around town. Securing her bicycle in the rack, Cari felt a raindrop on her hand. She looked up to see a cloudy sky. Nothing out of the ordinary, yet. But she wasn't going to wait around outside for a storm to begin.

She thanked the person opening the door for her.

"You're welcome," a familiar voice said.

Cameron Larke's grin matched hers as she passed him.

"What are you doing here?"

"I come here during my lunch break sometimes."

Cam went to the library during lunches? That was maybe not shocking, but unexpected.

"You here to see your nan?" he asked.

Carissa nodded. Then, she recalled his help the other day and hope lit up her eyes. "Did you find out anything else about Badb Catha?"

His brow furrowed a moment before realization dawned on his face. "The Raven, right. No, sorry. I've been swamped with work."

Carissa wasn't sure what work a chauffeur could be swamped with, but she suspected the mayor had him running around on all kinds of errands for him. Carissa and Cameron passed the checkout counter, the computers situated in front of the front windows, and the main office, heading to the circular helpdesk area in the center of the library.

Carissa turned right toward the nonfiction stacks, where she thought Nan might be since her shift hadn't yet started. She looked up at Cam, thinking this was where they would probably part ways.

"That's okay," she said. "Maybe Nan's found something on that, too."

Cameron kept following her, showing no sign of leaving. "Too? What else were you looking for?" He stopped in the aisle and stood against the bookcase to let a woman pass by.

So did Carissa, but for a different reason. "Mrs. Harbridge?" she asked.

"Cari, hello," Mrs. Harbridge said. For a woman whose son was in the hospital, she looked strangely happy.

"How's Timothy?" Cameron asked. Carissa didn't wonder how Cameron knew about Timmy's condition. It was just the ways things worked around Moss Hill— everyone knew everything about everybody.

Chaos in the Countryside

Mrs. Harbridge exuded happiness. Her freshly whitened teeth were showcased by her grin. Her eyes moistened. "He's alright. He is at home with Mrs. Alcott and her brownie."

Carissa disliked how she said 'Mrs. Alcott' so formally, instead of acknowledging they were actually good friends, or how she referred to Gilly by fae type instead of by name. She wasn't going to argue with her about it, though.

"I'm glad to hear it." Carissa genuinely meant it.

"That's great news," Cameron added.

Cari was a little perplexed at how he'd improved so quickly. According to Barnaby, he would still need a few days. She opened her mouth to speak but was cut off by Mrs. Harbridge.

"It was the strangest thing, actually." There it was. One never had to ask Mrs. Harbridge too many questions. Whatever she knew was always quickly relayed to the ears of whoever was listening. "The doctors said there was some kind of poison in his system from the ants." Mrs. Harbridge didn't acknowledge the abatwas. "They said he'd have to stay another day or two for it to clear out. We left him maybe all of ten minutes while the doctor provided his update. When we returned, three birds were sitting on his chest. Mr. Harbridge swatted those filthy things away and closed the window. Not a second later, Timmy sat up and told him not to hurt them. He says they healed him." Mrs. Harbridge waved the two square, hardcover book she was holding. "Now, he insists on reading all the books there are on brown birds. Heaven knows in Moss Hill they are not overfunded for nonfiction books. I'll have to get Mr. Harbridge to contribute. In any case, Timmy will be wanting these as soon as possible." She brushed past them as they said goodbye.

Mrs. Harbridge buying a book for her recovering son seemed like a nice thing to do. Cari knew her well enough to see she had left her son and come out to get the books herself for precisely the purpose of personally telling everyone about his recovery, instead of having them hear it from Mrs. Alcott.

Carissa and Cameron both moved to the side to let Mrs. Harbridge pass by and came back together once she was gone.

"Magical healing birds." Cam shook his head. "Now, I've heard everything."

Carissa pursed her lips. If Cam thought the magic birds were strange, he probably couldn't handle everything else going on in Moss Hill.

"So, what were you looking for?" Cam asked.

"Some information on nature faeries," she explained, and he followed her to a table in the back where, sure enough, Nan was perusing a bunch of old books. There must have been three open ones and five closed ones sitting on the table.

"I've already gone through those." Nan pointed to the stack of five and bypassed any kind of greeting as Carissa walked up.

"Any luck?" Cari asked.

"Only enough to confirm some types of fae and what I told you last night, especially about the sidhe." Carissa and Cameron both sat down. Nan continued, "All faeries are tied to nature, more so than humans. Every fae, of any type, shares a heritage with sprites and elementals, but the big folk, like humans, have more freedom to live away from nature."

"What do you mean? So, sprites aren't free?" Cam inquired.

Carissa thought she could explain this one. "It's like how you and I need water and air. Sprites need flowers, herbs, soil, and sunlight. They need to be near nature."

Nan added, "And nature needs them. They regulate the elements. It's a balance."

"So, how does a sidhe fit into this?" Carissa asked. "I've never seen one regulating nature."

"No, but you've seen them affecting nature. Their homes, for instance, are made from the earth."

That was true. Humans cut wood and pounded nails to make homes, but the fae homes were crafted as if the forest itself molded to their will and the earth was inviting them to stay. Sidhe lived in mounds no other fae type was allowed to see. But, based on what she'd heard of the giant redwood where the Sidhe Council met, their homes must be elaborate and more beautiful inside than anything a human could build. Carissa could see how all fae had a connection to nature, and given more thought, for the sidhe, this could be especially true.

"Still," she said, "I don't understand how one could affect the weather that much."

"They can't—at least, not regular sidhe," Nan said. "The only type I found was the ban sidhe."

"Banshees?" The gears in Cari's head were turning. "Cam, like the Badb Catha."

"Right." Cam scratched his head. "Okay, so I know the banshees are the ones who wail at funerals, or so they say. I've never actually heard one. But what are they, exactly?" His cheeks were a little red. As a Mossie who claimed to have some fae heritage, he should have known more about the fae. Still, he never claimed to be part sidhe, only part greggd anwn, a type of water fae, so Carissa let it slide without teasing him.

"Widowed sidhe." She couldn't keep the tiniest hint of a smile from her face, but she did try to explain without a condescending tone. "Sidhe have long lives."

That might have been an understatement; as far as Carissa knew, she'd never heard of a natural sidhe death. She went on. "Since they live so long, sidhe widows are rare. Their grief when their spouse dies is supposedly beyond their ability to control."

"Do you think this Badb Catha is in Moss Hill?" Cam asked.

Carissa thought about it. If she was this Raven Corvus, then Miss Morgan had hinted she was trouble. Could she be causing the events in Moss Hill? But, then why would she send Chaos? Why warn anyone at all? Unless Chaos was a spy and Corvus was just toying with Carissa? She frowned. That made no sense. As much as Chaos was a handful, Cari believed she really was there to help.

"I don't think so," she responded.

"Do we have any banshees in Moss Hill, then?" Cam inquired.

The only one Carissa had ever heard of was when she was little, about age ten. She recalled the mayor at the time had died. People reported hearing the cries of a banshee. Cam probably didn't remember because that was well before he'd had an interest in any local events besides sports.

"When Mayor O'Brien passed away," Carissa said. "That was the last time a banshee was heard in Moss Hill."

"Yes," Nan added. Her eyes looked far away off to the side, remembering. "There was wailing heard at the O'Briens' that night. It was a frightful sound. George O'Brien was a good man. All of Moss Hill was in mourning." Nan sighed and closed the book gingerly. "The last thing I read," she said, "was that a ban sidhe's grief becomes strong enough to affect their tie to nature. They can affect the area around them, whether or not they're aware of or in control of what they're doing."

"That makes sense." Cari leaned forward, speaking in low tones. "I thought I heard a wailing last night at the pub."

"The pub? Like, Second Street?" Cam leaned back. He swallowed and made his voice and expression as flippant as possible, which only showed Cari he was obviously bothered by something. "What happened?"

Cari explained about the pixies, and Cam bent in closer. His face was nothing near the nonchalant vibe of a moment ago. His eyes examined her like she was ill. "Are you alright?"

"Yes, nothing happened. Not to me, anyway." She decided not to tell him about Chaos. He would only look at her with more concern, and she found his expression a little unnerving. Even Nan never looked at her with so much concern. And that included age eight when her elf-light first caused her to move too quickly and she had ended up at the bottom of Crescent Drive with her bicycle on top of her. Her parents, as usual, had been away at the time.

Nan's shift was starting, and she had to leave. Carissa took her place, poring over the book, and Cameron helped as much as he could before he excused himself to go do whatever he had come by to do.

She saw him walk over and talk to the part-time library assistant, Tilly Brier. Cari's eyes kept glancing between the text and Cam. He seemed to speak with her a little longer than was necessary to ask for a book. The next time she looked up, he'd disappeared.

She read line after useless line until she gave up and left. She spent the better part of the afternoon looking through various parts of town, mostly gardens, and spreading the word among a few of the brownies and elves she knew. No one had seen Chaos, not even Barnaby. That was the last straw—if that leprechaun hadn't heard anything about her, no one in town would have. Cari gave up and traveled toward home, defeated. Against all hope, maybe Chaos had found her way back there.

Chapter 12

Tea and Tales

The wind picked up as Carissa traveled down Greenfield. Moving against it slowed her journey, but she trudged up the hill to her front gate. She clambered off her bicycle and made her way down the drive, only to stop in her tracks at the sight of a short figure cloaked in black huddled at her door.

The person was short enough to be a brownie. Maybe it was Gilly, Cari reasoned, wishing that would be true. She neither needed nor wanted any more surprises.

"Gilly?" Carissa's timid voice carried through the wind. It was meek, but the person had heard it. The figure turned and folded its hood back behind its thin ears.

"Miss Morgan?" Cari corrected herself. "What are you doing here?"

"The question," the brownie said, "is what was your nature faerie doing in my garden?"

Carissa's eyes widened, and her face lit up. Miss Morgan held the unconscious sprite up in her cupped hands.

"Chaos!" She nearly dropped her bicycle but caught it just in time to haphazardly lean it on the side of the house. She raced up the doorway and allowed the two inside.

Cari took Miss Morgan's coat, leading her to the sofa in the front sitting room. Under Miss Morgan's instruction, she lay Chaos on a bed of tissues and bundled her up. The brownie sat without taking in any of the room's décor; in fact, she barely looked at anything except Chaos. She rattled off a list of ingredients; Carissa didn't even know what for. She assumed they were to help the sprite. She gathered the spices Miss Morgan required into a coffee filter and tied it. Then, she put a pot of water on the stove, to warm, not to boil. Miss Morgan was very precise in her directions.

"What are the spices and water for—some kind of tonic?" Cari asked. As an apothecary, she hadn't come across a tonic with those ingredients before.

Miss Morgan looked at her like she was the slowest student in the class. "Tea, what else?"

"Tea?" She didn't want to scoff at Miss Morgan, mostly because the brownie intimidated everyone in Moss Hill despite her size, but her lips tugged back anyway. Cari released a frustrated breath without crossing the line into disrespect. She hoped Miss Morgan hadn't heard it that way, at any rate.

"Doesn't Chaos need something?" she whispered. "She's not well."

"Haven't you got eyes?" Miss Morgan demanded.

"Not well! She's sleeping."

Cari put a hand on the tissue, adjusting it to have a look at Chaos. The sprite rolled to her side. Her mouth was open slightly, her eyes were closed, and she made a soft chiming sound, the nature faeries' equivalent to snoring. She was alright. Carissa's breath came out in relief this time. She'd only met Chaos the day before, and already she was surprisingly attached. She felt she owed Miss Morgan her gratitude for saving the sprite.

Cari's smile lingered. "Thank you, Miss Morgan."

The brownie grunted. "The thanks is that tea you seem not to be serving."

"Right." Carissa let Miss Morgan's curtness slide. She got up and poured the water into a cup, dipping the makeshift teabag into it and thinking. She was too happy to dwell on Miss Morgan's rudeness, but she did wonder what had made the brownie this way. Had she always been so rude? Had something happened to make her pass her misery on to everyone?

If Miss Morgan had been a sidhe instead of a brownie, Cari would suspect she was the fae affecting the weather. That wasn't possible, though—was it? Yet, Chaos just happened to be in Miss Morgan's garden? It seemed unlikely.

Never mind the fact it was the Everlys' garden. Brownies didn't have gardens of their own. They were house fae, staying with other families—humans, generally—and usually amiable to the residents. It was true brownies tended to think of everything their human family possessed as their own, so it wasn't so odd she referred to the Everlys' garden as hers. But why was

Chaos there? Had she gone there on her own? Or had she been taken there against her will?

Carissa never thought she would have Miss Morgan drinking tea in her sitting room. Still, she handed her a cup of the warm liquid, and they sat, awkwardly on Cari's part. Though, Miss Morgan seemed right at home.

Cari expected Miss Morgan to tell her about how she'd found Chaos, but it seemed she was perfectly content to sit there until her tea was finished. Once or twice, Cari made to ask her a question, only for the old brownie to wag a finger in the air, signaling that she needed to wait.

Finally, when the tea was finished, Miss Morgan wiped her lips with a beautiful, white and green, embroidered handkerchief clearly inscribed with the Everly "E." Folding it carefully and placing it back into some invisible pocket of her frock, Miss Morgan finally spoke.

"She was healed by three birds, brown, white, and black. And that is how I knew."

Miss Morgan was always cryptic. Her meaning wasn't entirely clear to Carissa, but three birds? That sounded familiar.

"It was three birds that cured the Harbridges' son, Timothy." Carissa spoke rapidly, connecting the dots.

Wrath shot from Miss Morgan's eyes. At first, Carissa thought it might have been the volume of her outburst that earned her that look. But Chaos was still sound asleep.

No, Miss Morgan was a fae, and even though fae themselves tended to interrupt others, they hated when others interrupted them. Cari put a hand to her lips, and the heat rose in her face. "Sorry," she mumbled.

Miss Morgan titled her chin up, then gradually brought it back down. All was forgiven. The brownie restarted. "Three birds are a sign of Cliodhna, the first of the ban sidhe. She was always a vengeful, ill-tempered type of person."

Carissa forced her eyebrow to stay down, but she took note of the irony.

"She even cast a spell on her own sister," Miss Morgan continued, "all for jealous spite of sister's joy in being engaged to Chieftain O'Caimh. She was capable of many terrible things, but she could be a force for good as much as evil."

The way Miss Morgan spoke, it was like she knew her. But the first banshee must have lived centuries ago. Miss Morgan couldn't possibly have been that old, could she?

Carissa kept listening with rapt attention.

"Perhaps nature herself punished Cliodhna through MacLir." Miss Morgan looked her right in the eye. "She lost her love Ciabhan after he was killed by Manann MacLir."

"MacLir?" It all clicked together. Carissa stood as if a jolt of electricity shot through her legs. She paced about, which was difficult to do in such as small space between the chair, the coffee table, and the steps of the foyer.

She'd seen Cleena with three birds that first night at City Hall. Cleena's rage at the very mention of MacLir's name made more sense in light of this. It seemed impossible for Cleena to be that old, but if she were a sidhe, she'd have the same lifespan as one. Now that

Carissa thought about it, something about Cleena had seemed out of the ordinary for a human. Not just her actions, but her whole essence seemed different. Perhaps it was not unreasonable after all for her to be this Cliodhna of legend.

Carissa stopped in her tracks before she could wear a hole into the rug. Her mouth opened to share her epiphany with Miss Morgan.

"I think I know who it is. I think she's here in Moss Hill," Cari said.

Again, Miss Morgan looked at her with the weary eyes of an old-fashioned schoolmarm, the kind that thought dunce caps were appropriate. She took her cane and lifted herself off the sofa. She looked at Chaos and then up at Carissa.

"Yes, she is." The brownie had apparently expected her to make that connection a while back. "She does have a conscience, but she has to be reminded of it. The pleas of an innocent woman saving the people she loves. That's the only thing that will stop her."

Miss Morgan heaved herself up the steps and opened the door. Carissa moved to help her, but the brownie didn't need, nor apparently want her assistance. She left in the stormy weather just as Nan was driving up. Carissa would have offered her a ride, but between once glance at the driveway and a look back at the yard, she was already gone.

She hadn't thanked Carissa for the tea, but the information she had shared and the fact Chaos was safe now was thanks enough. Carissa walked over to the faerie, still sleeping soundly on the table. Somehow, she was sure that Chaos landing in Miss Morgan's garden was not a coincidence. This clever sprite had more to her than met the eye.

Chapter 13

Danger and Discoveries

The howling wind didn't relent all night. Carissa tossed and turned. She was uncomfortable no matter what position she lay in. When morning rolled around, she woke far earlier than normal, prepared, and left before anyone else was awake. At least, that was the plan.

Downstairs, the main cabinet was open, and several herbs and spices were strewn across the shelves and counter. Carissa, mouth agape, took giant strides to the kitchen and looked inside the cupboard, expecting to see a pixie tearing up the place.

It was just Chaos, sitting on the edge of a shelf, swinging her legs and contentedly munching on rosemary. Upon seeing Carissa, she wiped her mouth, wide-eyed, and hid the herb behind her back. It popped out from over her shoulder, making the effort humorously ineffective.

"Chaos." Carissa tried not to get upset this time. Chaos was here, she was safe, and she was living up to her name. Cari closed her eyes and breathed. When she looked again, the sprite stood, moving her eyes around innocently and twiddling her thumbs.

Carissa almost laughed, which helped in tempering her tone. She bent, bringing her face close to the nature faerie. "Here's what we're going to do. I will fix us some breakfast if you promise to stop raiding the cabinets."

Chaos brought two fingers up to her chest, making a crisscross over her heart. Carissa wasn't very familiar with it, but assumed it had a meaning like "cross my heart, hope to die."

She accepted Chaos' promise and prepared the food. When the three were done, including, Nan who'd come out of the room after the fiasco was all cleaned up, Carissa made her way to the door.

"Wish me luck." She grabbed her purse.

Chaos flew a few inches in front of her face, pointing out to the back garden. Carissa knew precisely what she wanted this time. "Oh no, Chaos, you're staying home and getting your rest."

"Why doesn't she go with you?" Nan asked from the other side of the hallway.

"Seriously? She was missing for a whole day and night."

"You said yourself she was getting Miss Morrigan—"

"It's Miss Morgan, Nan."

"And without the information she gave you, you wouldn't have been able to figure out Cliodhna was the one responsible. Maybe the nature faerie knows more than you realize."

Chaos nodded furiously. Carissa looked between the two. The advice might have been right, but it was hard to take seriously with Nan getting the names all mixed up.

"Cleena probably is Cliodhna, but that only makes her more dangerous."

"She healed Chaos," Nan argued.

Carissa put a hand on her hip. Two seconds later, she removed the hand and crossed her arms. Nan wasn't budging for all the argumentative body language Cari could muster.

Carissa shrugged and sighed. "I don't know how to protect Chaos if I take her with me."

The sprite bridged the four-inch gap between them and patted Carissa on the head.

Nan smiled. "I think she was sent to protect you."

Cari relented against her will. She ignored the fear that this was only putting Chaos in danger. Instead, she trekked through the house, twice—once to gather up the chocolate cosmos and again to take it out the front door to her bicycle.

Carissa secured both the plant and the nature faerie in the basket and rode down the hill that was the neighborhood of Crescent Circle. Starting at Greenfield, the journey was odd. The weather seemed almost comical, sunny and windy and cold and rainy, back to sunny again by the time she reached the shop. Chaos looked up at her with her tiny eyebrows raised in an *I told you so* kind of way, to which she rolled her eyes to relay, *Fine, I get it.*

At the shop, Carissa was surprised by the sight of the mayor's Mercedes parked outside. Cameron hopped out the front door with a smile and ran around the side, opening the door for the mayor himself. Carissa took out the chocolate cosmos and met her visitors at the front door.

"I'll hold that," Cam volunteered as she reached into her bag for the key.

Carissa expected an argument from Chaos, but the sprite had camouflaged herself into the flower. Before she could ask the mayor the reason for his visit, he reached out for a handshake.

The mayor beamed. "Thank you!" Belkin shook her hand with vigor. "Rolin has agreed to the tourism increase, and the sidhe has said...." He deepened his voice to the authoritative tone of a sidhe. "The human town is not our concern." He laughed heartily.

Carissa's lips thinned to a disingenuous smile. She held the door open, allowing the visitors inside. "Glad I could help." She took the plant from Cam's care and walked it to the back counter. The mayor followed, going on about how this change would benefit the town. But would it? Carissa felt that perhaps this was the very change in Moss Hill that Raven Corvus had been warning her against. Would it invite more dark fae to their town?

She didn't know how the town would handle even the one misguided fae. What would happen if several came to shore? Carissa didn't bring it up. It wasn't her call to make.

The mayor practically burst with joy. "So, it's official. Mr. Goodfellow asked MacLir to ferry down from the mainland tonight to sign the agreement for the restoration projects—and not a moment too soon. The *Everly Express* will be ready for its maiden trip tomorrow afternoon, so he can ferry back in style. Everything is falling into place." He clapped and rubbed his hands together like a kid anticipating cake.

Carissa replied, "That's great. But, um." She looked down at Chaos, debating what to do. *How exactly does one say, "By the way, I think someone working for you is really an ancient fae who's responsible for all the crazy weather, and, oh yes, did you see the pixies the other night? I think she did that, too."*

The worst news of all was that MacLir himself was coming. It couldn't possibly be Manann MacLir. As far as Cari knew, Manann was human and had passed on a long time ago. She had heard of a Lir in history—a sea god of old. MacLir could mean "son of Lir," but fae tended not to have last names in the same way as humans. No, since the person she'd loved was human, his killer was likely human, too.

But Cleena was beset with grief. In her mind, all that mattered was MacLir was the name of her mortal enemy. If news had reached her that any MacLir was coming to town, Carissa didn't know what Cleena would do.

Mayor Belkin went on as if he hadn't heard her. Cari couldn't think of what to say even if she could get a word in edgewise.

"We're holding the christening ceremony tomorrow at five p.m. You are, of course, invited." He grinned and examined the store like he was seeing it for the first time. "It's been a while since I've been in here." He glanced around. "I've forgotten if you have a restroom."

Cari cleared her throat. "Oh, no, I'm sorry. Gooseberry next door has one, though."

"Excellent," the mayor said. "I could also use a cuppa. This'll be a change, Cameron. I'll get you a coffee, if you want. Limited time offer, what do you say?"

Cameron smiled and put a hand on his neck. "I'd love one. Do you think I could have a minute first?"

Belkin tiled his eye line to Carissa. A knowing smile spread across his face. He tipped his head and walked out the door, whistling.

Cam laughed and turned back to Cari. "He's in a good mood."

Carissa looked down. Out of the corner of her eye, she could see Chaos stepping away from the plant to become visible again.

Cam scratched the back of his head. "So, sorry I didn't help you more at the library yesterday."

Carissa bit her lip. "That's okay," she said too quickly. "Actually, I really need to talk to you about that."

He tilted his head and put both hands on the counter, leaning her way. "Why? What did you find?"

She told him about the legend of Cliodhna, including her supposed watery end in Glandore.

"Glandore?" He propelled himself off the counter.

Carissa was taken aback by his startled reaction. Her eyes questioned him from underneath upraised eyebrows.

"That's strange, are you sure?"

"I am. Why?"

"Yesterday, we had an employee who practically went off when she heard about the deal with MacLir going through. Three guesses what her last name is?"

Carissa opened her mouth in a disbelieving grimace. "I'll give you the first, too. Cleena Glandore?" When Cam confirmed it, she shook her head. Cliodhna had chosen her new name for anyone to see. Miss Morgan must have known who she was all these years.

"But, if she could pass as human, is there a chance MacLir is the one of legend, too?" She had to ask.

"I don't think so." Cam's chin cut a definite line in the air as it moved. "Magnus MacLir is pretty famous where he's from. I heard the mayor and John talking all about him and his father as business tycoons. He seems human enough to me."

Carissa exhaled. At least they had only one fae to deal with instead of two. She couldn't relax, however.

"I think Cleena's dangerous," Carissa said. "I think she's the one behind all this weather and the other weird happenings." She didn't care to elaborate.

Cam nodded. "I'll tell the mayor. We'll detain her when she comes in." He put one hand flat on the counter halfway between them. "Don't worry." His eyes met hers. "We'll handle this."

His words didn't reassure Carissa much, but she tried to give a grateful smile. Even if the mayor took his warning seriously and they somehow managed to detain Cleena, there was no one among the human Mossies with even as much faerie magic as Carissa. Cameron didn't seem put off by any doubts. He strode out the door with determination fueling his steps. Pushing the door aside, she saw him turn toward Gooseberry with single-minded focus.

Cari hadn't realized she was gripping the counter so tightly her knuckles were turning white. She let go and looked down. Cari noticed Chaos leaning off the side of the flower pot with both hands on her chin. She had a dreamy look in her eye that turned into a nod of approval when she looked at Carissa.

Chaos in the Countryside

"What are you smiling about?" Cari allowed the annoyance to seep into her tone as she put a hand to her hip. She smiled anyway to show she was teasing. Chaos rolled her eyes like a teen and sat back by the stem of the plant. Carissa didn't have time to give much thought as to what that was about.

Instead, Maren walked into the apothecary shop at the perfect moment. "Did I just see Cam leaving?" Her smile was as devious as Chaos'. "He's looking good today."

This time, Carissa did the eye-rolling. She picked up her purse and the chocolate cosmos and passed Maren in the aisle. She had to get fae assistance if she wanted Cleena stopped. As well-intentioned as Cameron was, she couldn't rely on human intervention to stop a ban sidhe.

"Something's come up," Cari said. "Can you mind the shop for a few hours?" She bit her lip. "Better make that all day, maybe."

Maren's puzzled eyes scrunched down, and her nose crinkled. "Sure, why? Is everything alright?"

Carissa nodded, feeling her heart begin to race. She faked a smile and made her way through the row of healing tonics.

"It will be," Cari said.

She walked outside to see the clouds thickening and merging overhead. It was strangely unnerving and reassuring at the same time. She'd have to race against foul weather to get to Vale Woods, but when the sidhe guards looked up to that ominous sky, they would have to agree to help.

Chapter 14

Fate and Fatalities

Varick was the first one she spotted. At first, he brushed her concern aside, but the clouds were spreading, and the Vale Woods would be affected soon. Chaos pointed this out, practically shouting at Varick—or performing the hand-waving equivalent of a shout. Carissa pulled her lips to the side in dismay when Varick listened to the nature faerie over her.

He took Cari and Chaos' complaint to the head of the sidhe guard. The tall, dark-haired, muscular sidhe came directly to speak to her. He scratched his beard as she talked, and his eyes gave her the distinct feeling that she was talking to someone old enough to make her seem like an infant in comparison. He treated her about the same as one, but he was taking her seriously, at least.

One mention of the name Cliodhna changed the guard's demeanor. He—whatever his name was, he obviously thought her too beneath him to give it—agreed without further hesitation to send a squadron.

Chaos in the Countryside

They traveled with Carissa into Moss Hill, but at the town line, outpaced her on their horses, fae-touched with magic as they were. She panted and exuded more elf-light than she'd ever done before. It was too exhausting to maintain.

She felt a little ridiculous shouting "Wait!" at the guards. Only one of them turned around. He didn't actually stop but did her the courtesy, if one could call it that, of circling around her and ordering, "Your part is over. Return to your work." He rejoined the group, leaving Cari behind.

She and Chaos, finally in sync with their feelings, both steamed the rest of the way back to the shop. Carissa practically hit the door when she re-entered the Seelie Tree Apothecary. Maren leaned backward slowly from behind a row of shelves to see who had entered.

"Is the emergency over?" Maren asked. Her tangled brow suggested she knew it wasn't.

"No." Carissa pounded the ground with each step and launched the chocolate cosmos with enough force to cause Chaos to redirect her anger. She turned a raging glare toward Cari. Carissa winced but didn't have the emotional energy to apologize.

"If everything's not okay, you don't have to stay. No one's even come in, the weather's so bad outside," Maren suggested.

As if on cue, Cari's phone rang with all the messages she'd missed while she was in Vale. It had been about two hours, and Cam had sent three texts. She clicked to open the app.

Cari hadn't read the first word before pulling her neck back as a startle response. She felt two miniature hands on her shoulder. Chaos was peering over at the phone as if she could read.

Carissa's eyebrow shot up. Maybe she could read. She'd never heard of a nature faerie who had that skill, but then, Chaos was different. Carissa discarded the notion as unimportant for now and scrolled through the messages.

> *9:20 a.m.—Cleena called in sick. Belkin sent officers to her house.*

That was unsurprising. One probably wouldn't go to work on the same day they had planned to murder their arch-nemesis. Only it wouldn't be her arch-nemesis, would it? Carissa clicked the next text.

> *9:45 a.m.—Not there. Conducting a discreet search around town.*

Cari wondered if he meant the officers, or if he, personally, was searching for Cleena. She felt lightheaded. She pulled the stool from the back corner to the counter.

"Uh-oh." Maren ventured over. "You never use that chair. You have to tell me what's wrong."

Chaos in the Countryside

"Shush, give me a minute." Carissa didn't see Maren's response, but her shadow loomed over her.

Cari suspected that if she looked up, she'd see a look to rival her Nan's *you have until the count of three* expression.

She checked the time on her phone. It was already noon. She couldn't imagine there were many places left in town that they wouldn't have checked. She texted Cameron with one sentence.

Check the docks.

She lifted her gaze to Maren. Sure enough, there was that hand-on-hip, annoyed stance about her. "Sorry," Carissa started. Another text from her phone cut her apology short.

Already did. Not there.

She began texting back. Maren's diminishing shadow told her that her assistant wasn't waiting around for her attention. Her phone rang in the middle of the sentence.

She answered, "Cam, where are you?"

"City Hall."

"Any luck finding Cleena?"

"Not yet."

Cam's calm tone increased the volume of Cari's voice. She wavered as she spoke. She pressed the phone tighter to her ear.

"She's angry about MacLir. She'll go to the water," Cari said.

"We checked already." Cam was incredibly patient not to sound annoyed by her insistence, but she couldn't think of anything else.

"Where are they looking now?"

Cam hesitated. "They're not," he said. "The mayor called off the search."

"What? Why?"

"She hasn't done anything yet, Cari."

"She's causing this whole storm."

"The mayor's not convinced of that."

"Isn't he worried she's missing?"

"She called in sick, and we've only searched a few hours. She's not technically missing.

Carissa rolled her eyes, knowing full well he couldn't see it. She hoped the sidhe would be more thorough in their search. She glanced at Chaos, who stared out the window.

The sky was gray, and now rain was pouring.

It dawned on Carissa. "Maybe she doesn't need to be on the shore. Maybe the whole point is to turn the weather bad enough that a ferry boat can't make it to shore. If so, the weather will get a lot worse this evening."

"Oh." Cam sounded like a school kid who just realized he'd forgotten a project was due.

"What?" And there was Cari, sounding like a cross teacher.

"I should've mentioned. Magnus MacLir sent a lawyer on an earlier ferry. He's arriving this afternoon to sign the contracts."

Carissa's eyes could have popped out of her head. Firstly, the first name "Magnus" confirmed it was not the same MacLir from Cleena's past. Secondly, if it wasn't MacLir on the boat, why was there still a storm outside?

"Could Cleena know this?"

"No. Oh, actually yes." Cameron corrected himself. "She's the city recorder and notary, so she might have been notified via email. That is, if the mayor didn't tell his secretary about your suspicion of Cleena."

Carissa bit her lip. "What are the chances he did?"

"It was your theory, Cari. I hate to say it, but I think the only reason he sent anyone searching for her in the first place was your father's position on the Fae Council." Cam sighed.

A scratching sound came at the door. She looked to see Maren opening it. In the next second, Cari heard two things. The first was Cam saying, "I'm pretty sure Cleena knows the ship's arrival time was changed. I'm not sure she knows it's the lawyer and not MacLir who's coming."

The second thing she heard was Maren's high-pitched, motherly, smothering voice saying, "Oh, what an adorable kitty!"

* * *

FOLLOWING A CAT through town during a storm wasn't Cari's first choice. Yet, oddly enough, it seemed like a good idea at the time. The last two times she'd seen Aibell, the cat had taken her straight to Cleena. It was her best bet to follow the feline now.

Three streets down, Carissa felt somewhat silly. She was relieved when Aibell brought her to the sidhe guards, right at the end of Fourth Street, by the pier. What was even more surprising was that the sidhe followed the feline without hesitation. It was like they trusted the animal more than they did her.

She could stew on that later. She fell in line with the guards, who didn't argue about her presence this time. Aibell led her down the beach, confirming her suspicions. The beach was devoid of people. Even on the short ride over, the storm had gotten so rough that Cari imagined anyone waiting for a ferry boat would have taken shelter indoors. The ferry itself might have turned around if it weren't already in Cleena's grasp.

Carissa was grateful Chaos hadn't insisted on bringing the chocolate cosmos. It would have been torn apart in this weather. Chaos herself shouldn't have come. She shivered and clung to Carisa's hair for dear life. Cari picked her up, trying to protect her and keep her warm.

Carissa's eyes scanned the shore. The torrent of rain colliding with the earth and the wind slashing at her face made it difficult to see. She put up her hand to shield her eyes and blinked to locate the source of the storm. The sounds of Varick and the sidhe guard stomping over the rocky ground was drowned out nearly completely, except for the occasional sliding of stones as they tried to keep their footing.

"Head to the pier!" the lead guard ordered.

Chaos shook in Carissa's hands. Looking down, Cari saw she was shaking her head and pointing to the rocky shore near the bottom of Aisling Mountain. At once, she understood—Cleena was going to lure the boat into the side of the mountain. Her vengeance would be a shipwreck. She'd have no mercy on anyone aboard.

"No!" Carissa called out to the sidhe. "She'll be in the rocks! Trust me!"

A paw touched her leg. Did the cat seem relieved she understood? Seeing Aibell shivering and feeling Chaos sneezing in her hand, she realized the two of them couldn't follow. Looking down, she saw the nature faerie using her light magic to create a sort of shield from the storm. It kept flickering in an out as she lost her strength.

Carissa looked around, spotting a nearby food stall. It must have been closed up in a hurry due to the change in weather. There was about an inch underneath the side of it, large enough for a cat to sneak under.

"Aibell," she shouted, even though the cat was right in front of her. "Go with Chaos and take shelter." The cat turned in the direction she was facing, then looked back at her to nod in understanding.

Chaos couldn't even protest, given how much she was shaking. Carissa placed her onto the cat's back. The sprite was just able to grab the fur when Aibell sped off toward the shack.

At least Chaos had taken shelter out of harm's way. Carissa couldn't do that. She'd come this far. Learning from her nature faerie friend, she used her elf-light to create a type of protection around herself.

The guards had moved away, disregarding her. She kept on. They didn't order her to follow, and she knew at her core Chaos was right. The sidhe would find nothing at the pier.

Once she'd made it over to the rocks, she found the object of her search. Cleena stood against a boulder just below her, holding both hands out to create the storm.

"Cleena!" Carissa tried to get her attention but couldn't be heard over the storm. "MacLir isn't on the boat!" Cari raised her voice to nearly screaming. "You'll be killing innocent people!"

Cleena's arms twitched. She must have heard her. The thunder and lightning eased. It was still raining, and the water crashed violently against the rocks. Carissa could see the ferry coming into view. She imagined the captain on board had realized by now the danger they were facing. The wild waves would reach the boat soon and pull it into the jagged land.

Cleena's whole body leaned toward Cari, only a few centimeters. Her eyes were on the ship, but Carissa had her ear. At least, she hoped she did.

"I know what he did was wrong. But that MacLir is dead. He died a long time ago."

"He's not dead! He can't die!" There was madness in Cleena's tone. Grief, rage, pain, all of it and more dripped from her cracking voice.

"His *grandson*," Carissa emphasized the word, "is not on that boat. And even if he were, there are others whom you have never met, whom you don't even know, whom you would be killing for the sake of vengeance. You would be guilty, just like MacLir is guilty of causing death and pain."

"They chose their path! They chose to work with him."

Carissa's mind raced. She was seeing them as the soldiers in MacLir's army. Her view on reality was distorted, and her emotions were running too high to see reason.

She tried a different approach. "What about their widows? What about the pain you'll cause to them? Do they deserve to suffer because their men chose to come here? Will it matter if these men came against their will or not?"

Cleena flung her hands down, lifted her open mouth to the sky, and screamed. She cried out so loudly that, as a reflex, Cari's hands shot up to her ears and pressed. It was dizzying in intensity. Carissa had never heard anything like it but recognized the sound.

That was the cry of a ban sidhe.

Once death had touched them, a widowed sidhe was said to know when death was near. Thereafter, each time the widows felt death approaching, they were said to cry in despair like no other being on Earth. So, their cries became known as an omen of death. The legends of the banshees had begun with this woman. Carissa hoped to lay them to rest here and now.

The queen of the banshees sank to her knees. The weather was still violent, but the rain had eased enough to see her more clearly. Varick hastened toward her, but Cari held up a hand. The guard's stern expression told her he disapproved, but he also heeded her request. She approached cautiously, until she was close enough to speak without shouting. Carissa knelt, making herself small enough not to be perceived as a threat. She tried to use as comforting a voice as possible.

"They're at your mercy. Their lives are in your hands. If you don't stop those waves, you'll be responsible for all their deaths. Manann MacLir was a killer. Are you?"

Tears streaked her face. She reached an arm out in front of her, and the ocean began to settle. The unnaturally dark clouds started to clear. It was already morning, though it hadn't seemed that way until now. In the rising sun, Cleena's ocean blue eyes were glowing with the sheen of exhaustion and grief.

The sidhe soldiers crested the top of the rocks. Varick lifted the woman, gently but firmly grasping her upper arm with one hand. The guards surrounded her, effectively blocking Carissa from having any more to do with their capture.

She couldn't help but feel sorry for Cleena. She hoped they would show leniency in determining her punishment for all the chaos she caused. A sudden sense of urgency overtook Cari as she realized she'd completely forgotten Chaos and Aibell.

The cat was probably still hiding under the stall, but with Chaos, one never knew. The spunky sprite was danger-prone and had already proven not to be one to sit out during a catastrophe. If she'd left the shelter, who knows how hurt she could be?

Carissa dashed to the stall to find Aibell outside of the cart, peering underneath and purring. She was stretching out a paw toward something but stopped when Carissa arrived. She swooped behind Cari and gently pushed her forward. Carissa bent all the way to the ground.

Sure enough, under the stall sat the nature faerie, huddled with her wings wrapped around herself. Carissa put her palm under the cart, and the sprite crawled in. Once she was in her hand, Carissa could feel she was still wet and shaking. Comparing Aibell's slightly damp fur to Chaos's soaked body, she put together the picture of what had happened.

"You left the cart to follow me, didn't you?" Carissa's tone chided.

The cat meowed affirmatively. Chaos swiveled to face the other way and opened her wings to block herself from Carissa's view.

"Don't be like that, Chaos." Carissa eased into a gentler, but still firm voice. "I'm only upset because I don't want you putting yourself in danger like that."

Chaos turned to show her side profile. Her magnificent wings stretched behind her, and she held her head up high with her eyes closed. No sooner had her arms crossed in front of her than they moved to her face as she sneezed. Fairy dust blew from her little mouth and nostrils, and she sniffed and wiped with the back of her palm.

Carissa found it too cute not to laugh, but that only made Chaos turn red and hide behind her wings again. Cari shook her head, still smiling.

"Come on, let's go home. We'll have a nice cup of tea and some biscuits."

Slowly, one wing came down. Chaos' little eyes peeked upward, but Carissa pretended not to see it. She let the sprite take her time coming out of her wings on her own terms.

"You can come, too," Carissa addressed the cat, but Aibell was nowhere in sight.

Her eyes traveled over the bay. Down at the pier, the boat was landing. Trotting right to the dock was a little blur of white. That cat was strange, alright. Aibell sat straight and tall, as if waiting for someone on the boat. Carissa never had found her owner but had a feeling the feline knew where she was going.

Chapter 15

Bon Voyage to Banned Fae

The Seelie Tree Apothecary couldn't stay closed all day. Maren was happy to open without her, but Carissa had to go down there at some point and get her day's work in. So, at around nine, she opened the front door of the shop, carrying a chocolate cosmos in her arms. She made it clear to Chaos that this wasn't going to be a daily thing, but today, she didn't mind that the sprite insisted on tagging along.

Inside the shop, she was surprised to see Miss Morgan standing at the back counter, apparently giving Maren a lecture on how she was drying herbs incorrectly.

Maren gave Cari a "thank god you're here" look, and Miss Morgan lifted her chin up and stopped speaking when she entered.

"Good morning," Carissa said.

Chaos glanced between all of them and then took off from the flower to Miss Morgan's shoulder. The brownie's eyes moved toward the faerie, though her stance was unmoved. After a moment of listing to Chaos—or rather, looking at Chaos' miming—Miss Morgan responded.

"Well, of course, she did. Why thank her? She's half-fae. It's her duty." Chaos hugged Miss Morgan's shoulder. It didn't make the brownie any friendlier. She patted the sprite. "Okay, okay, that's enough of that."

Miss Morgan snatched the little brown bag of her purchases from the countertop and twisted on her cane to face Carissa and the front door. She took three measured steps forward.

Carissa thought she might pass by without another word, but the brownie stopped. She leaned upward on her cane.

"Heed the letter. The Unseelie are no small threat. Be aware and be ready." She struck her cane against the ground, causing Cari to literally jump back. Miss Morgan clacked and stomped cane and leg all the way to and out of the front door.

Maren rolled her eyes with some comment about the brownie's battiness, but Carissa took her warning seriously. If the last few days had taught her anything, it was the legitimacy of Raven Corvus's note. The only problem was, she didn't know how to be ready for dark fae, and she would be the first to argue that she was the last person who should be preparing for that task.

She regretted not telling the sidhe but wondered if telling them now would only make things worse. They might reprimand her for not bringing it to them at once, or dismiss it because Corvus was a surname, indicating it had come from a human. As Mr. Morely had pointed out in the city hall meeting, the sidhe didn't listen to humans.

Chaos in the Countryside

Throughout the day, several Mossies, unaware of what had transpired last night, asked Cari and Maren if they were going to the pier to see off the *Everly Express* on her maiden voyage. The mayor would be giving a speech, and several of the prominent residents of the town would be going.

Maren replied right away in a chipper, high-pitched tone, "Sounds like fun."

Carissa considered it but did not give a definite answer. She thought it best to get to Vale as early as possible.

Right at four o'clock, she locked up, said goodbye to Maren, and put the chocolate cosmos into the bicycle basket. Unlocking her bicycle, she made not two turns of the wheel before she saw Barnaby across the street.

"Are you going to the pier?" Barnaby asked.

He was fae, so she couldn't just give a quick response and dash. She sighed and turned, cycling across the street and waiting just a few paces in front of him. As he caught up, Chaos twisted around and gave her an evil eye.

"Sorry," she whispered, realizing the large circle would have had a dizzying effect on the small sprite.

Barnaby appeared at her side, placing his cap on his head and repeating his question. Without giving much away, she relayed her plans to travel to Vale. The leprechaun laughed off the idea.

"If you're looking for Rolin, even the head elf is attending the ceremony."

She hadn't thought of the possibility that some of the Vale residents would be at the pier today as well. She doubted the sidhe would be there. Though, come to think of it, if the head elf was attending, at least some of the sidhe guard would be sure to accompany him, as well.

"If you can make it," Barnaby went on, "a bunch of us are meeting at Second Street Pub afterward." The leprechaun waved and moved on.

"Maybe. Thanks, Barn." She looked down at Chaos. "Well, what do you think?"

Chaos looked right toward town and left toward Vale. The fresh sea air and celebration won. Chaos pointed right.

"Hold tight," Carissa said. She raced along the hilly terrain. Toward Second Street, the crowd increased. She found a spot in the parking racks for her bicycle looked down to the beach. It wasn't all of Moss Hill, but the turnout was impressive. After a minute of arguing with Chaos that she was not going to hold a plant throughout the Mayor's speech, she finally got the sprite to leave the chocolate cosmos behind.

The nature faerie lifted herself onto Carissa's shoulder and hid at the crook of her neck. The breeze was refreshing but problematic, as Cari felt a tug at her hair where Chaos tangled herself into her locks.

"Ow, careful!" Carissa whispered.

The sprite lifted herself and floated alongside her a minute. When she started flying away, Carissa attempted to call her back. "Sorry, Chaos. I didn't mean it like that. *Chaos.*" She followed, a little annoyed at the sprite's sensitivity.

But Chaos didn't just fly away. She soared straight to a man and woman mingling in the crowd. The woman smiled as Chaos settled into the palm of her hand.

"Hello, Chaos." She looked at the faerie.

Chaos in the Countryside

Carissa gasped upon hearing the woman's recognition. Her first thought was this blonde haired, slender-framed, blue-eyed woman was Raven Corvus, but a shining object at her neck told a different story.

It was the same locket that had been worn by the cat.

"Aibell?" The name barely escaped Cari's disbelieving mouth.

The woman's smile had an unmistakable familiarity about it. Though up to that point in her life, Carissa would never have thought a cat and a human could possibly resemble each other. She almost forgot that a man was standing next to the cat-turned-woman.

The man extended a hand. "Collin O'Caoimh," he said.

A spark of recognition shot through Carissa's face. She shook his hand and her chin at the same time, grinning. Her eyes met Aibell.

"You're Cliodhna's sister?" Cari smiled, with a tinge of red highlighting her cheeks. Of course, it all made sense. The curse had been a spell that turned her sister into a cat. Carissa was a little embarrassed she hadn't figured it out sooner. Chaos twirled, laughing at Carissa's dimness. She fluttered beside Aibell. It was good to see the sprite stretching her wings.

Aibell smiled at the sprite. To Cari, she said, "Once or twice, I thought you suspected I was a cat sidhe."

"Cat sidhe?" The words felt strange put together on Carissa's tongue. She assumed it was what it sounded like—a sidhe turned into a cat. Even growing up with fae all around her, things like people turning into cats was still relegated more to the realm of myth and legend than reality.

Aibell titled her head. She looked at Cari like a thin envelope held up to the light, and she was reading what was written inside.

"You haven't embraced your fae side, Carissa Shae. You'll have to learn if you want to protect Moss Hill."

Disbelief pulled every muscle in Cari's face down in sync with her lips.

"Why me?"

An electronic noise turned everyone's heads toward the boat. The mic check's echoing failure reverberated over the sand. An announcer came on, apologizing as he fixed the microphone on the temporary stage at the pier.

At the top corner of her vision, Carissa saw Chaos flying in the direction of the stage. She zoomed so fast Carissa didn't even have a chance to call her back. She pursed her lips. When would Chaos learn not to run off like that? Who was she going toward, anyway?

Chaos disappeared as she neared Rolin and several sidhe guards at the forefront of the assembly. To Carissa, they clearly looked like fae, but she could see how a non-Mossie might think they were just uniquely dressed humans. Collin regained the group's attention.

"John," Collin said.

Carissa shifted her gaze beside Collin. John went up behind the man and clapped him on the back. "Are we ready to go?" He seemed to notice Carissa at that moment and said, "How are you feeling?"

"Better." Her face reddened. "I should explain about the other night—"

"No need." John held a hand up. "Maren explained everything. I hope that cat is alright. I heard you caught it later. I'm sure the family was happy when you returned it."

Carissa and Aibell shared a glance. "Yes, I think they were." She beamed. Cari silently thanked Maren in her mind. Then, her eyebrow rose. She glanced between the two men. "How do you know each other?"

John answered, "Mr. O'Caoimh is a lawyer for MacLir industries. We just signed the agreement today. We'll...well, *I'll* return once we've got the final go-ahead from Mr. MacLir."

Collin took that as a cue. "We should be going, or the boat will leave without us." He kissed Aibell on the forehead and picked up the luggage. Carissa hadn't even noticed the bag on the ground. It seemed light for two people. Then again, Cari imagined spending years as a cat would mean Aibell had few items to take with her.

"I'm sure we'll be back to visit the O'Briens from time to time," Aibell said.

Cari smiled and felt the warm glow of familiarity. Aibell had been the O'Briens' cat? How coincidental was that?

"We'll see each other again." She reached out and hugged Carissa. It surprised Cari, but she returned the embrace, happy she had helped that mysterious cat sidhe after all.

Aibell and Collin wandered through the crowd toward the beach. Carissa knew they were giving her a moment alone with John. She bit the corner of her mouth, worried about Chaos getting lost in the multitude of people.

"So," John said, "I know we didn't get to have a proper date, but maybe when I get back, we could try again?"

She looked down gathering courage. Looking back at him, she said, "John, I like you, but I just don't think that we—"

He put both hands up this time. "Say no more. I understand." He offered a handshake. "Friends?"

She placed her hand in his. "I'd like that."

John joined his companions and walked up to the dock. Carissa followed. The three of them quickly merged with the crowd. She had wanted to ask Aibell about her sister's fate but felt she couldn't do it in front of John.

Cari walked until she got to the pier near the mayor's stage. She put a hand to her eyes, surveying every direction around her, but it seemed she'd lost Chaos. She would have kept wandering the area, but the mayor's voice came over the microphone.

"Ladies and gentlemen, my fellow Mossies," the mayor's speech began. "Today is the start of a new period in Moss Hill's history. Up until now, we've hidden away from the rest of the world, barely noticed. Today, as we christen the first of the new ferryboats, we open our shores and our hearts to all future visitors of Moss Hill. Let the ceremony begin!"

Cheers and smiles washed over the sand as the captain gave his speech, invoking the sea to watch over the vessel and casting the name *Everly Express* into the records. He poured champagne into the water and shared the rest of it with the Everlys and others on the stage. Plenty of Mossies across the beach had brought their own libations.

Someone near Cari offered her one, but she declined. She was still worried about Chaos. With the speech done, she weaved through the crowd to look for her. Not three steps in, she stopped, startled upon realizing Varick now stood right beside her.

He put a hand to his shoulder and brought it down to reveal a certain nature faerie, who hopped happily from his palm to Cari's. Chaos flew right up to Carissa's neck and grabbed onto her hair again. She pulled it as she turned. Cari winced, but the pain of the hair pulling was nothing compared to the worry during the faerie's absence. She thanked Varick for bringing her back.

"You should watch her more carefully," Varick replied. His attention moved back to Rolin, who was on stage, shaking the mayor's hand. Or, he might have been watching the Everlys beside them. He began to step away.

Carissa's question stopped him, "May I ask what happened to Cleena?"

Varick's expression had far less variance to it than Cari had ever seen on any being, human or fae. He turned to her, stoic as usual, and simply replied, "She is on the boat."

Exile? Carissa wondered. "Are there guards watching her?"

Varick tilted his head toward Cari, eyes still on the stage. "She's traveling alone."

Carissa couldn't help but jolt her eyebrows up in concern. "Aren't you afraid she might go after MacLir or even attack her sister again?" She shook her head. "Don't get me wrong, I'm glad she got some leniency, but letting her go completely free? She could still be dangerous."

Varick finally looked from the stage to Cari. "I highly doubt she'll be of harm to anyone in her current condition."

"What condition?"

He moved away, not answering.

If she didn't know Varick better, she could have sworn he wore a smirk on his face. He made his way back to the stage. Several sidhe guards converged near Rolin. Completely protected, the head of the Fae Council left, presumably for Vale Woods.

Sighing and frustrated at the fae's pleasure in being mysterious, Carissa put a hand above her eyes and set them toward the boat. The *Everly Express* was a beauty. Its pristine, white hull glistened in the sun. On the top deck, Cari could see some of the passengers, including Aibell and Collin. She waved, but they didn't see her.

Movement by their feet drew Cari's attention. There, a beautiful, orange-coated tabby clutched the railing. It seemed like it had waited until it caught her eye. Then, it lowered its paws and stood in the same regal way as another cat she once knew. Carissa waved again, this time at her. The feline nodded, as if accepting both her consequence and Cari's goodbye.

"Well, Cari," Barnaby's voice called her back. "You're here, splendid! Come and join us."

Chaos flew down to Cari's fingers and tugged her by the hand. She turned, smiling. To Barnaby and Chaos, she said, "I'll be right there."

Looking back at the boat, she couldn't see Cleena anymore.

"Bon voyage," Cari said to the air.

Chaos hovered to her side and gave a salute before zipping over to Barnaby. Carissa giggled at the sight.

Chaos in the Countryside

She gave one last look at the departing ship, then turned to join her friends, which, gladly, now included a brave little sprite named Chaos.

Sneak Peak of Book 1: Herbs and Homicide

Summary: *In the small town of Moss Hill, customers of all kinds visit Carissa Shea's Seelie Tree Apothecary Shop. That includes tall and short, young and old, human and faerie. Being half-elf, half-human herself, Carissa personally knows and cares for them all. So, when a grumpy brownie—a type of house faerie—named Miss Morgan dies in her shop, Carissa is devastated. As she learns more about her customer's death, she realizes Miss Morgan might have been the only thing standing between the Seelie, faeries of light and goodness, and the Unseelie, faeries of darkness and evil. On top of it all, the sidhe guard, protectors of all fae residents, rule it murder and name Carissa as a suspect! Now, she must prove her innocence and find the real culprit before it's too late— not just for her, but for all of Moss Hill.*

Excerpt:

Perched above the pedals of her blue beach cruiser, Carissa Shea navigated the winding paths of the friendly neighborhood of Crescent Circle in the early morning hours. Her light pink blouse flared around her. The locket at her neck pressed against her chest in the wind. The red-haired, fair-skinned woman with dark brown eyes and slightly pointed ears was unmistakably human and undeniably fae, depending on one's knowledge of the otherworldly people.

And no one knew the otherworld better than the residents of Moss Hill.

Want more great content?

Hi, I'm Astoria Wright, author of the Faerie Apothecary Mysteries. I hope you've enjoyed this novella prequel to The Faerie Apothecary Mysteries.

The Faerie Apothecary Mysteries

Chaos in the Countryside
Herbs and Homicide
Remedy and Ruins
Elixirs and Elves
Charms and Changelings
Potions and Panic
Talismans and Turmoil

To keep up to date about this series and others by the author, check out the website:

www.astoriawright.com

Sign up for the mailing list for updates and freebies available only to members!

A Note from Chaos:

Do you like this book?
I hope you do.
Please do me a favor
and leave a review!

Thanks for reading!